KU-289-242

EAST SUSSEX COUNTY COUNCIL
WITHDRAWN
2 4 AUG 2024

03379519 - ITEM

No Second Chance

The name Cole Adams was known to too many people – lawmen, outlaws, kin of folk he was said to have murdered during violent robberies.

But was he guilty of these crimes or had someone been using his name? Riding innocently into town, beard-shaggy and buckskin pockets bulging with gold nuggets, he walked right into trouble.

There were bullets with his name on them – and, always, the shadow of a noose hanging above him.

No Second Chance

CLAYTON NASH

A Black Horse Western

ROBERT HALE · LONDON

© Clayton Nash 2007
First published in Great Britain 2007

ISBN 978-0-7090-8474-7

Robert Hale Limited
Clerkenwell House
Clerkenwell Green
London EC1R 0HT

www.halebooks.com

The right of Clayton Nash to be identified as
author of this work has been asserted by him
in accordance with the Copyright, Designs and
Patents Act 1988

EAST SUSSEX
COUNTY LIBRARY

EAST SUSSEX COUNTY COUNCIL

2 4 AUG 2024

03379519		
HJ TW	595756	
F	£11.99	
11/07	PEA	

HA1 12/08
HAS 6/09

Typeset by
Derek Doyle & Associates, Shaw Heath
Printed and bound in Great Britain by
Antony Rowe Limited, Wiltshire

CHAPTER 1

LONESOME

The claim jumpers struck just before sun-up and that was their mistake.

The man known as 'Lonesome' had decided he had had a bellyful of this isolated valley. He had enough nuggets and alluvial gold dust for what he needed and he still suspected that a big rich vein wound its way just a few feet from the end of his tunnel. All the sign was there: he would need better tools to tackle it, likely even blasting powder.

He could come back, *would* come back, but right now he needed a break: nine months of living wild, Indians sometimes friendly, other times after his scalp or weapons, half-starved most of the time because once colour began to show he simply didn't want to stop and spend time hunting for something to eat.

He recognized it as gold fever, was somewhat surprised, for he had always thought he was one man who was immune to that affliction. But when nuggets fell at his feet with every third or fourth swing of the pickaxe – hell, he had actually felt drunk! Just as if he had downed a jug of redeye. *Crazy! Giggling! Dancing, for Chrissakes!*

So, after starting a minor rockfall, enough to cover the last few feet of the tunnel where he had been digging, he took it as a sign: end it here – for now.

He decided then and there, left his tools in the tunnel and made his way out into the fading daylight. Just time enough to pick off a jackrabbit, maybe even a young deer not yet experienced enough to know it was dangerous to venture into a valley with only one way in – and out.

He was lucky: shot a deer right on dark, and ate well. Too well. His belly had been used to hardtack and indifferent grub for too long. An hour after eating he lost the entire meal, spent an uncomfortable night with griping pains in his belly and little sleep.

He was still awake when he heard them coming.

He had deliberately placed dead and half-dead brush across the path, enough so that it couldn't be avoided. It would have to be moved aside, and the dry branches and leaves would rasp and snap no matter how careful the intruders were.

He had long ago built up a small mound of earth behind which he had spread his bedroll. Now he took up his Winchester, the butt wired up where it had split after he had been forced to use it as a club on a leaping cougar after a shell jammed in the ejector. The rifle hadn't worked too well after that but it picked off the first intruder in the grey light, knocking the man down in a twisting fall across the narrow trail.

His two companions left him where he fell – he wasn't likely to rise again anyway – and dived for cover. He could hear their startled voices and some nervous curses, half-smiled, although the movement of his lips was lost amongst the dusty, bushy beard that hid most of his face. His fairish hair hung in greasy strands down to his shoulders: a visit to the barber's would be one of the pleasures he would allow himself once he returned to civilization.

'You can't get past us, Lonesome!' one of the men called. 'We got the trail covered! Just leave us your gold and you can be on your way.'

'You're already on your way – to hell!'

Lonesome knew where they were hiding: he had arranged that there were only two places that would give cover. He worked his way past his earth mound, dragging his greasy buckskins across the ground which he had kept clear of gravel so it wouldn't crunch when he moved. They started shooting, wasting their lead, pouring it into the raised earth, actually giving him extra cover with the dust the bullets created.

Two steps up and he was in amongst a nest of boulders that gave him a view of their hiding-place. A red-haired man, hat hanging down his back by a thong, lifted up enough to draw a bead on Lonesome's sleeping place. His finger squeezed the trigger at the same instant as the prospector fired. Red smashed backwards with a clatter, his worn, dusty boots sticking up between two rocks, unmoving.

The third man didn't waste time: he leapt to his feet and made a helter-skelter run back along the narrow trail. Standing, the man in buckskins glimpsed the ground-hitched horses then saw the man skid, almost fall, but straighten, drop his rifle, and keep on going. In the grip of panic.

He was lunging for the nearest horse, a dumpy man in ragged clothes. His hands just touched the reins of the nervous mount when Lonesome's bullet slammed between his shoulders, driving him solidly against the horse. It reared and pawed the air. The luckless claim-jumper caught the down-plunging hoofs and they finished him even if the bullet hadn't done its work.

The man in buckskins stood, rifle cocked and ready, but apart from drifting gunsmoke and fading echoes, there was nothing to indicate that there had been a gunfight here.

After checking all three and making sure they were dead, the prospector buried them by jamming the bodies into a crevice and collapsing a cutbank over them. Two of the horses he turned loose, but kept a black gelding he liked the look of.

Then he packed his gear and left the valley by mid-morning, forking the big black, leading his pack-mule, his leather poke of gold tied around his waist under his dirt-stiff buckskin pull-over shirt.

Those claim-jumpers must have worked mighty long and hard to locate him. They were the first in the nine months he had worked this valley.

First and last. He would cover his tracks so well that no claim-jumpers would ever get a second chance at stealing his gold. No one.

The town was called Gallant. Why, he neither knew nor cared. Thunderheads were building to the north as he rode in and the air was sultry.

He had never been here before, had made a deliberate detour across the state line, so that if anyone had been watching for his reappearance they would be twiddling their thumbs a hundred miles away. Lonesome wasn't lonesome at all, really. He could stand his own company. Sure, he talked to himself a little, maybe to his mount, cussed out the pack-mule, but he didn't much miss the sound of human voices.

That was because he had never really been free of them, growing up with five sisters and a grandmother. During the war, for six years he was surrounded by voices: bawling orders, screaming as their owners died or suffered hellish agony, speeches by politicians trying to rally a beaten army. Afterwards, dozens of sharks were trying to sell him something or dupe him in some way – talk, talk, talk – endlessly. Silence was precious! It was one of the things he had cherished most during a period of his life that he had been trying to forget for five years.

He had decided that, when the country had settled down after the war, he would find himself some prove-up land in a lush valley somewhere and live in a cabin which he would take pleasure in building: he liked working with wood. And if, one day, he should feel the urge for a wife and children, that sounded okay, too: but he would make sure he could support and feed them before he dived into that kind of thing.

But it all happened faster than he had prepared for. And ended much sooner than he wanted.

Cowpunching paid too little: he never saved a cent – there was always someone or a group eager to help him spend his few bucks. But he didn't want to think back to those years – not now. There were buildings in the distance. . . .

All too soon the sounds of civilization – such as it was, this far west – began to close around him. The clatter of buckboards, creaking wagons, shouting men – and women, laughter, the grunting efforts of a couple of men fighting outside a saloon, the whinny of a horse – he was back and it was by his own choice.

What gold he had would buy him a little pleasure and the rest would go on suitable land. Looked to be some good cattle country in the hills behind Gallant, green, well-watered. The town looked tolerably prosperous, with several stores fronting Main, a couple of saloons. Then he spotted a bathhouse; soap and hot water, then a shave and haircut, a good meal and a soft bed to sleep in. He looked around quickly for the livery stables.

The hostler wanted payment in advance; the prospector didn't blame him but he noticed the way the man was looking at the gold he proffered. 'Strike it rich?'

'That'll be the day.' He handed the man a small nugget. 'That take care of my packhorse and mount for a couple days?'

'Well – sure. Just about do it.'

Lonesome knew by the man's hesitation that it was

more than enough. 'Stow my gear till I come for my horse?'

'Sure thing. It'll be safe with me.'

'No use going through it. I carry what gold I've got with me.' He let him see his rifle, a good Winchester that he had taken from one of the dead claim-jumpers.

The liveryman's smile vanished and he nodded curtly, saying, 'We got a tough sheriff in this town.'

The man in buckskins said nothing, walked through the big double doors and made his way to the bathhouse.

He had three changes of bathwater before he felt clean, his hair and beard looking twice as huge now that they were fluffed up. He had a Mexican boy buy him some clothes while he washed: two shirts, one blue, the other brown-and-white check, two pairs of Levis which he had to return as he had lost more weight than he had figured during his long sojourn in the hills. He changed into new corduroy trousers in a back room of the store and picked himself a hat with a curl brim and dented crown before buying tobacco and a couple of neckerchiefs. He didn't bother putting one on as it would be hidden by the bushy beard.

The storekeeper looked at the several small nuggets of gold Lonesome held out in his calloused hand. 'That's way too much, feller.'

'Pick the one you figure will cover what I bought.'

'You'd trust me to do that?'

'Go ahead.'

The storekeeper hesitated and chose a tear-drop

nugget about the size of his thumbnail. 'This is the closest. I can give you credit for the extra.'

'Sure, I'll be around for a few days.'

Feeling mighty strange in his new outfit, the prospector found his way to a barber shop and took his place on the bench with three other waiting men. They all looked at his beard and hair, the barber working, but casting sidelong glances, too.

'Been a long time since I've been in a town.'

'Can see that. I'll have to charge you a quarter to get rid of that bush.'

The man shrugged. 'Do what you have to. Just don't be too greedy.'

The barber straightened, face stiff. 'I have the reputation of being an honest man, mister. If you've any doubts, I won't miss your custom.'

The prospector grinned but it wasn't noticeable amidst all that hair. 'My apologies, barber. Like I say, long time since I been among people.'

The men who had been before him had their haircuts and shaves, then waited to see the barber trim his hair down and get rid of that beard. His face emerged, pale from no sun reaching the skin for so long: it was a square-jawed face, with a hawklike nose, wide mouth. The eyes were grey-blue now the brows had been trimmed and the head of hair was the colour of flax, gleaming with a spray of bay rum. The barber had even massaged his scalp, trimmed the hair in his ears.

'Man, you looked like a shaggy bear when you come in. Now seems to me, you turn side on you mightn't even throw a shadow!'

They all laughed at the barber's comment, including the prospector. 'Aim to eat a mite better from now on.'

Their faces sobered when he paid in gold.

The barber lived up to his reputation, had a small set of scales and weighed a little gold dust to cover the cost.

'Here, you'll need to sharpen your scissors as well as your razor.' The man handed him a small pea-sized nugget. 'I'm obliged – even feel kinda – human again. Gents, if you're in the saloon bar while I'm there, I'll buy you a drink.'

The trio were already making for the door when the barber said, 'Friend, if you don't mind a little advice – don't flash that gold around – keep it under cover as much as you can.'

'I'm going to the bank now and change it into cash.'

'Bank's are stingy. Try the assay office first – get a valuation so you'll know if anyone's tryin' to cheat you.'

The prospector did this and the assayer, just using his knowledge on a visual check, told him he had likely $200 worth – maybe a little more; he wasn't certain about the gold dust, but if he liked to wait he could weigh it precisely. The prospector shook his head.

'Would you give me two hundred right now?'

The assayer hesitated. 'Well, I don't normally buy unless there's something special about a nugget – but, yes – I'll give you two hundred – even.'

The man counted out coins and greenbacks and

13

wrote in a book, swivelling it around towards the prospector. 'I'll need your signature. The department's a stickler for rules. But you needn't fill in the space that says "Location Gold Found". No one expects you to give that away.'

The prospector wriggled his fingers, held the pen awkwardly. 'Been a while . . .' he said apologetically and then laboriously wrote his name in the column indicated by the assayer, who turned the book towards him again. He squinted, trying to make out the words.

'Is that Adam Cole?'

'Cole Adams.'

'Why'd you put the last name first?'

'Sort of a habit I got into once. Wife of the rancher I worked for kept the books, said it was easier to have the names in alphabetical order by writing the last name first. Dunno how she got on with the fellers who could only make their mark, not even write their own names.'

The assayer was sober now and seemed to Adams a trifle nervous. He closed the book with a snap. 'Well, enjoy yourself in town, Mr Adams. Gonna be here long?'

'Maybe.' He touched a hand to his new hat's brim. 'Obliged for your help.'

The assayer watched him leave, then hurried to the front door, closed it and turned the cardboard sign in the half-glass panel from OPEN to CLOSED.

He went out the rear door, and started to run.

Cole Adams bought the three men from the barber-shop their drinks and after a whiskey and beer chaser, felt the alcohol hit him harder than he'd figured.

Still, he might have expected it, having been so long without potent liquor out in his valley. He had no intention of getting drunk; maybe later he might have a few extra drinks and perhaps the company of some fallen dove – but not right now. *Maybe not later, either, he told himself, remembering without conscious effort . . .*

He went back to the general store and asked the man behind the counter, Mel McKinley, for a Colt pistol and gunbelt. 'Ammo, too, of course.'

'Well, we got a good selection of pistols. Used as well as brand new. Depends how fancy you want it.'

'Not fancy. Just good enough to hit what I aim at.'

The door opened and a tall young ranny dressed in grey trousers and a lighter grey shirt stepped in. There was a brass star pinned to his shirt pocket and confident blue eyes settled at once on the newcomer.

'You Cole Adams?' A little belligerence in his tone as if he expected trouble. Maybe even wanted it.

'That's me.'

The lawman's gaze shifted to McKinley. 'He armed when he came in here?'

'Had a rifle. I said I'd look after it for him . . .'

Adams stiffened when the lawman suddenly drew his sixgun and cocked it. 'Come on.'

'Where?'

'Jail. Now come on!'

'Wait a minute! What the hell you holding a cocked gun on me for? I've just arrived in town and—'

15

'And you're gonna regret it as long as you live – which won't be too damn long if I have anythin' to say about it.' The lawman jerked the gun barrel impatiently. 'Now, I ain't gonna tell you again, Adams. Let's move! I can take you in dead or alive. You choose. And fast!'

CHAPTER 2

JAILED

The man in grey was Deputy Renny Kendrick, son of the sheriff, Nate Kendrick.

The older lawman was partly bald with grey tufts of hair over both ears. His face was creased and weathered but you could see the likeness of Renny there. He glanced up from several wanted dodgers he was holding.

Renny stood to one side, covering Adams with his Colt, glancing at his father occasionally. *Looking for approval? He did seem kind of nervous.*

He was also taking sly looks at himself in a fly-spotted wall mirror, turning his head this way and that as if checking out the lie of his wavy brown hair.

'You must be loco usin' your own name in this town.'

Adams was still mighty puzzled, sitting in a chair where the deputy had slammed him down as soon as they entered the law office. 'Why? I ain't ashamed of my name.'

Both Kendricks snorted, exchanging glances. 'You hear that?' the sheriff asked. 'Man who's killed seven people, held up as many stages, robbed express offices and rustled God knows how many cattle, ain't *ashamed*! Well, you damned well oughta be, feller! It'll be interestin' to see how you feel when they tighten the noose around your scrawny neck!'

By now Cole Adams was feeling mighty alarmed, his heart pounding his ribs. He started to rise but the deputy hit him with the gun barrel where his shoulder joined his neck. It drove him down into the seat, hot pain burning a path all the way up and into his brain. He felt his eyes water.

'Christ! What the hell is this?' gritted Adams, rubbing his shoulder. 'You got the wrong man!'

'You're Cole Adams?'

'Yeah, I admitted that, but—'

'Then you're the man we want.' The sheriff shook the fistful of dodgers. 'You're wanted in three states, includin' this one – fact, includin' this here town!'

Adams frowned, slumping a little. 'I've never been in this town before in my life! I just came down outta the – outta the north, crossed the state line, and stopped at the first town I came to – here.'

'Your mistake,' gritted Renny. He seemed as if he was barely containing himself, that, without his father to control him, he might gunwhip Adams, even shoot him dead.

'Listen, I—'

The deputy back-handed Cole before he could say any more – and wasn't expecting Adams to come straight up out of the chair, butting him under the

18

jaw and sending him reeling. Adams went after him, grabbing for the man's Colt, but froze when he heard a gun hammer behind him clicking to full cock.

'You're a hair away from findin' out whether there really is a life after death, mister!'

Adams saw the sawn-off shotgun steady in Kendrick's hands, the sheriff's face set in hard lines, knuckle white on the finger curled around the trigger. Cole lifted his hands and Renny came off the wall, working his throbbing jaw. He swore once and hit Adams in the midriff, bringing a knee up into his face. Adams crashed to the floor in a corner and the deputy would have kicked him but his father snapped an order and Renny eased back against the wall, glaring at Adams.

'I'll see you in the cells later!'

'Never mind that,' growled the sheriff, motioning for Adams to sit down. Kendrick sat on a corner of his desk, the shotgun held across his thighs. 'You murderin' snake. I oughta blast you now, save the county the cost of a trial.'

'I'll do it, Pa!'

'Neither of us'll do it. I kinda fancy the notion of this son of a bitch sweatin' out a trial, knowin' all along he's gonna be found guilty and swing for his crimes.'

'What crimes? Hell almighty, I've been in the hills for most of the year, grubbin' for gold! This is only the second town I've been to in all that time. I bought some supplies in Redwood and never left my claim till—'

'Yeah, sure. I don't doubt you been in the hills somewhere, but not lookin' for gold. You were hidin' out with your gang, just comin' down to rob a stage or ride across the line to Drumhead and hit the express office or the bank. An' there's the railroad – let's not forget the two trains you held up – and the two crewmen and a caboose guard you shot!'

Adams could only stare, running the tip of his tongue over his lips. He shook his head slowly. 'You got the wrong man,' he said again, feelingly.

'Uh-uh. You thought that flour-sack hood you wore'd save you bein' identified, but one of your men let slip your name, didn't he? And the caboose guard heard him, didn't die from his wounds. He heard one of your men say "We better hurry, Cole!" An' then a kid brought your getaway mounts to the door of the express car an' said, "All ready. Mr Adams!" Guess you figured it didn't matter, expectin' the guard to die.'

'I swear I dunno what the *hell* you're talking about! If I – if I was loco enough to rob a train you think I'd leave anyone alive who could tell my name? Reckon I'd shoot the two fools who mentioned it anyway!'

The sheriff nodded. 'Yeah, well, that sounds like you, all right. But you slipped up. The guard lived long enough to tell your name. But I'd guess the ones who mentioned it ain't still livin'.'

'Dammit! *I'm innocent of all this*! I was looking for gold in the . . .' He stopped; even in this situation he hesitated to mention the name of the hills where he had found gold.

'Where?' asked Benny, rubbing his swelling jaw

now. 'Where you look for gold? You hit a bonanza, maybe. . . ?'

'No. But I got a couple hundred bucks' worth. Ask your assayer. He gave me cash for the nuggets.'

'And told us you'd signed the book "Cole Adams".'

'That's my name. I've admitted it, but I never did those crimes. I worked that gold claim alone.'

'Ever get – lonesome?' asked the sheriff with a shrewd look.

'Lonesome?'

'Ring a bell, does it? That was another name that was dropped durin' a hold-up. Ever been called that?'

'Sometimes – after I lost my wife, I was pretty much a loner for quite a spell.'

'Ever been in jail?'

Adams hesitated. 'Jail, yeah. Prison no . . . I was jugged in Laramie a few years ago. Put to work on a chain gang – a token sentence for beating up a son of a bitch who scared the hell outta my wife when she was pregnant and I was away from the cabin. He was on the run, wanted money and grub, was gonna take my wife hostage but I arrived back in time.'

'You kill him?' Renny asked.

'Not quite. But I left him pretty well smashed up and he got ten years on the rockpile. I aimed to be waiting for him the day he was released . . .'

'Son, you are only makin' things worse for yourself. See? You are violent, by your own admission. You got a killer streak in you. What happened to your wife?'

Adams's face set into sober lines. 'She died. The

fright she got brought on the baby. There were complications. Local sawbones was drunk out of his mind. So I had to drive fifty miles to the next town. All that jolting in the old buckboard and – we never made it. Damn wheel I hadn't gotten around to fixing – well, the spokes gave way, the buckboard overturned . . .' He drew a deep breath. 'I got out of it with some broken ribs and a busted leg.' *And a bunch of memories he still found hard to shake.*

The sheriff waited a moment. 'You the only one survived?' At Adams's nod, he glanced at Renny whose face was blank. 'Guess that made you kinda – bitter, huh? Mad at the world?'

'Hell, Pa, don't go makin' excuses for him! He's a bloody murderer and thief and—'

'Shut up, Renny. He'll pay for his crimes. You see, Adams, your name was mentioned in a couple other places you hit: Wells Fargo in Cheyenne, a bank in North Dakota. Your gang were kinda free with your name.'

Adams flicked his gaze from one man to the other. 'Don't that tell you anything?'

They stared blankly at him.

'Someone's setting me up! Dropping my name at all these places. You get anyone else's name to put on the goddamned dodgers besides mine?'

They stared back but the sheriff straightened and went back to sit in his desk chair, frowning slightly at Adams. 'Well, that could be, I guess, if you stretch a long bow. You got someone hates you enough to do that to you?'

Cole Adams was silent, his face showing nothing of

his thoughts. 'Guess not. Feller I beat up died in prison. No one else I can think of.'

' 'Course he can't, Pa! He's just stallin'!'

'That's what you're doin', son, isn't it? Aw, no need to answer. You're a smart *hombre*. All these crimes we got you down for were well planned, and you got away every time – leavin' no witnesses, except a couple times when you didn't make sure they were dead. And those men're gonna reach out from beyond the grave to hang you, feller!'

'For hell's sake! When were all these things s'posed to have happened?'

'Over about the last year or so. Just the time you claim you were all by yourself in some mystery mountains, looking for gold! Kind of a coincidence, ain't it?'

Adams said nothing.

' 'Course even if you told us where you were, if you were alone there'd be nothin' to prove you spent all that time there, would there? No one to back up your story.'

'I dug a tunnel into a mountainside. Must be thirty-some feet long. All shored up, too. I can describe it perfectly . . . and that took more than a couple of days!'

'You dug it all by yourself. huh?' Renny laughed. 'And cut timber to shore it up! Pa, we got us a mighty powerful man here! Have to be careful he don't yank the bars outta the cell!'

'I've had a bellyful of this snake,' the sheriff said abruptly. 'He made a mistake stoppin' off here. Maybe he did it to thumb his nose at us, you an' me!

He got away from us after he pulled the bank robbery that time – comin' back is just the kinda thing he'd enjoy doin'.'

'And sign my own name in an assay book when it's supposed to be on so many Wanted dodgers? Use your head, Kendrick. I'd have to be plumb loco!'

'I think you *are* plumb loco!' snapped the older Kendrick, standing now. 'Man who can kill in cold blood like you done sure ain't what I'd call sane! Lock him up, Renny. I'll have to send some wires to other sheriffs who want him, get someone down here to identify him.'

'And tell you how much the reward is?' Adams said sardonically. 'Feller who's s'posed to've done all the things you say, must have a big price on his head.'

'Shut up!' snapped the sheriff angrily.

Adams suddenly smiled. 'Ah, now I see why you're so riled; being lawmen just doing their job, you won't see any of that reward – or mebbe just a token few dollars!'

Renny's fingers dug painfully into Cole's arm as the deputy dragged him to his feet, backhanded him. 'Pa told you to shut up! Reward or not, you'll still hang!'

'How can anyone identify me if I'm supposed to have been wearing a flour-sack hood?'

'Don't worry none about that, mister. We'll have you all labelled and fitted up nicely for the legal boys so the judge'll only have to say where an' when you're gonna hang.'

Nate turned away in disgust, automatically placing the shotgun on a shelf to one side of his desk. Renny closed in on Adams, who suddenly spun in a blur of speed, smashing a fist down across Renny's forearm, numbing it completely so that the pistol thudded to the floor. Cole hooked an elbow under the deputy's jaw, sending him crashing across the desk, scattering papers, pens and ink-bottles as he sprawled.

The sheriff, older and stiffer, moved more slowly but he lunged for the shelf where he'd put the shot-gun. Adams heaved the semi-conscious Renny at his father. Both lawmen went down in a tangle. Cole spun towards the street door, reaching for the handle – and remembered how Renny had locked it before sitting him down in a chair for questioning.

The keys had been on the edge of the desk – and now lay somewhere on the floor amongst the scat-tered papers. He didn't waste time trying to find them. The other door led to the cell block so there was no escape that way.

He lunged for the shelf with the shotgun, but Renny staggered up and launched himself in a flying tackle, arms going about Adams's slim hips, carrying him into a cupboard. It rocked and toppled. It was the one where the sawn-off shotgun rested – which was now somewhere under the overturned cupboard.

Cole kicked the deputy in the chest and dived over the desk, shoulder-rolling amongst the papers and books, groping desperately for Renny's fallen sixgun.

As he searched, on hands and knees, Sheriff Kendrick stood up, a little blood on his mouth and one nostril, his Colt in his fist, cocked. 'Hold it right there, feller!'

Then he stepped around the desk and swung a boot against Adams's side. Renny staggered forward and got in half a dozen good kicks before his father hurled him back.

'That'll do for now. Put him in the last cell in the row. It's the draughtiest and leaks when it rains.'

The sheriff lifted his eyes to the ceiling and Renny grinned as they both heard the rumble of thunder.

'Gonna be a wet night, Pa,' the deputy opined.

'I hope so, son. I sure hope so!'

CHAPTER 3

THE GUN

Nate Kendrick had two more deputies, tough, hard-eyed, and curious. They came down the passage and stood at the bars of the cell, looking Adams over.

'Reckon it's him right enough, Ed?' the one with the frontier moustache asked. 'Kinda hard to tell.'

'Seems about the right size. Never seen much of him, to be truthful. I was in the privy when all the shootin' started at the bank and by the time I got my pants up far enough to run without trippin', the robbers were headin' outta town in a cloud of dust.'

'Yeah, well, I took a couple shots at 'em, thought I winged one, but never was sure. Hey, Adams. One of your pards stop a bullet in the leg durin' your getaway?'

Lying on the bunk, hands clasped behind his head, Adams turned slightly. 'I never robbed your lousy bank. Nor anything else your crazy sheriff has accused me of.'

Ed bristled. 'Quit that kinda talk!'

'Yeah, might as well, I guess. None of you half-wits are ever gonna listen to me.'

'Who you callin' a half-wit?'

'Don't see no one else but you and your pard.'

'You hear this sonuver, Hank. . . ?'

Before Hank could answer, Renny Kendrick came down the passage. 'What's all the damn yellin'?'

'This skunk's bad-mouthin' us, Ren!' Hank growled.

Kendrick stood close to the bars, his eyes cold.

'Let that go for now.' He reached inside his shirt and pulled out a folded piece of calico. He shook it out and the deputies looked startled when they saw what it was: the corner of a flour sack, with ragged holes cut in it for eyes and mouth.

'A goddamn hood!' breathed Ed. 'Just like them robbers wore!'

By now Adams was standing close to the bars, looking from the hood to Renny Kendrick. He said nothing although it was obvious that the deputy expected him to. Kendrick thrust the hood through the bars.

'Found it in the bottom of the warbag you left with Andy Perry, our livery man.'

'It's not mine. I've never seen it before.'

'Oh? Just carryin' around for a friend, mebbe?'

'If you found that in my warbag, someone planted it there.'

Kendrick arched his eyebrows, turned to look at the other deputies. 'Now, wonder why we never thought of that? Tell you what, you try this on and we'll see if it fits.'

28

'The hell I will! It could fit a hundred men.'

'But I want to see if it fits you!' Kendrick thrust the hood as far as his arm would reach. 'Now put it on!'

'Go to hell.'

'Get the keys, Hank.' Renny turned when the deputy didn't move and said more loudly and emphatically. 'Get – the – goddamn – keys!' He sounded like a school bully.

Hank hurried through to the front office and returned with the ring of keys. As Kendrick sorted through them and slid one into the door lock, Cole Adams stepped back into the centre of the cell. All three lawmen crowded in and advanced towards him, the door closed behind them.

He jumped up on to the bunk beneath the high, barred window, fists cocked and ready. The trio had done this kind of thing before. Ed feinted at Adams's legs and the prisoner jumped back, swung a kick. Renny Kendrick and Hank moved swiftly, Hank grabbing the swinging leg, Kendrick knocking the other one out from under. Adams crashed to the bunk and rough hands mauled him, dragged him upright.

Ed and Hank held his arms in such a way that if he struggled he was in danger of either breaking bones or tearing his shoulder ligaments. Half-doubled over he prepared for the beating he knew was coming his way.

Then the flour-sack hood was pulled over his head, twisted and turned until the eyeholes were at the front. He could barely see out of the ragged apertures, but he saw Kendrick spread his long legs so as to get a solid footing. The big deputy spat into the palms of his hands and then doubled them into fists. Adams watched every movement. But he should have been watching Kendrick's legs. The right one kicked out and the boot took him in the genitals. He groaned sickly, legs buckling, all his weight on his arms, searing pain surging through his shoulders. Kendrick grinned tightly and slammed his fists into the prisoner's ribs and midriff. He twisted the fingers of his left hand in the loose cloth of the point of the hood, yanked Adams's head back and smashed him in the face. Blood oozed through the calico at about nose level.

The big deputy set his legs again and sliced blow after blow into Cole Adams, the man's body rocking with each impact. Blood splashed on all three deputies, stained Adams's new checked shirt. He was barely conscious and Kendrick was breathing hard, sweat stinging his eyes. He brushed a hand irritably across his face, set himself again and hammered half a dozen blows into the sagging man.

'Hell, he's gettin' heavy, Ren!' complained Ed.

'He's out,' growled Hank. 'Let the son of a bitch fall.'

They released their grips and Adams sprawled on the stone cell floor, bloody and unconscious. Renny Kendrick sucked split knuckles, shook his throbbing hands.

'Got a head made of solid bone!'

'We better lay him on the bunk,' Hank said sounding worried. 'Nate finds him like this, he'll tear our heads off.'

'Nah. Pa'd just be sorry he wasn't here to get in a

lick or two himself,' Renny said, trying to sound brashly confident, but he grabbed Adams's legs and indicated the others should take him by the shoulders.

They pulled the blood-spattered hood off and threw him on the bunk, then left the cell, locking the door again.

'There's already lynch talk in the saloon,' Ed said quietly. 'Plenty folk are riled at this one.'

'There'll be no lynchin'!' snapped Kendrick. 'He's gonna stand trial and swing legal. Pa won't have it no other way.' He grinned suddenly. 'Which don't mean Adams mightn't walk into a door or fall down the steps goin' to the privy. And what happened to him this time? Tripped over his own feet, din' he, strugglin', tryin' to dodge puttin' on that hood? Fell flat on his face.'

He winked and the deputies nudged each other. Trust big Renny to find a way to make the murdering bastard suffer.

Tess Fowler turned her roan towards the hitch rail outside the law office. The two cowboys riding with her, slowed their horses, and as she dismounted she said, 'Give Mr McKinley the ranch order and then you can have a drink at the saloon. Just the one, mind. I won't be long here.'

She looped the reins over the hickory bar, hitched at her silver-buckled belt around her slim waist. She was wearing a white long-sleeved blouse with a calfskin vest over it, and denim work trousers pushed into the tops of dusty half-boots. Chestnut hair spilled in waves from beneath the weathered wide-brimmed hat. She removed the hat, shook her hair loose and held the hat in her hand as she entered the law office.

Nate Kendrick looked up from writing in a thick ledger at his desk. He set down his pen when he saw her, smiled and nodded as he stood.

'Got my message, huh?'

'Young Telmann said you have the man who robbed the bank and killed my father.'

'Yeah, the one who killed your pa, Tess. Cole Adams.'

She had a narrow face but a pleasant one, none of the pinched mouth or narrowed eyes of the dyed-in-the-wool spinster, although she must be in her late twenties and wore no wedding ring. Her grey-green eyes narrowed slightly and her full red lips tightened perceptibly, but she still looked a handsome young woman, even though pale with tension.

'You're sure it's him, Nate?'

'He admits it.'

'Admits the hold-up and murder. . . ?'

'Well, no – admits he's Cole Adams. 'Course he denies he held up the bank or shot anyone, but he's the one, all right. Renny even found a flour-sack hood in his warbag. Thought you might be able to identify him, seein' as you was there when it happened.'

'For Heaven's sake, Nate! There were four of them and they *all* wore hoods made out of flour-acks! I wouldn't know the man if he sat next to me in church!'

Nate Kendrick smiled crookedly. 'Which ain't very likely to happen. No, Tess, I figured maybe you got some idea of his size and general appearance. He's wearing a checked shirt like the killer was. You must've heard his voice, too.'

'I heard him yelling at the man who let slip his name, but that was muffled by the hood. I don't know, Nate. Much as I'd like to see Dad's murderer punished, I wouldn't want to make a mistake and identify the wrong man. I mean – it all happened so fast, and I was so shocked when Dad was shot down, right beside me, apparently without any reason. I didn't notice much after that. I was too concerned for Dad.'

Her voice betrayed her emotions and the sheriff fidgeted uncomfortably. 'Yeah, I savvy that, Tess. Sorry, din' mean to upset you. I just want to be sure we got the right man, too. But, if you could look him over – even if you can't recognize anythin' about him, well, I guess it makes no nevermind in the long run. He's gonna go on trial anyway.'

She was still reluctant but in the end agreed to look at Adams in his cell. *She doesn't really want to face the man who murdered her father*, Kendrick thought.

When she saw the battered and bruised Adams sitting on the edge of his bunk, dabbing at a cut alongside his mouth that was bleeding a little, she rounded sharply on the lawman. 'What's happened to him?'

'Nothin' much – he got rough with Renny and the other deputies, refused to try on the hood. Fought 'em when they tried to put it on him. You gotta let

NO SECOND CHANCE

these fellers know who's boss, Tess. Partic'ly a cold-blooded killer like this one. He ain't showed no remorse at all.'

Adams was watching her, trying to read her face. There might not be actual sympathy there, but she sure wasn't pleased to see the way he had been beaten: he filed it away. In his position, even the possibility of an ally had to be nurtured and ready to use at the right time. And she looked very uncertain about identifying him.

'They say I robbed the bank and killed some people,' Adams said to her quietly, coming to the bars. 'I've never even been in this town before today. I'm not the man they want, ma'am. That's gospel.'

She stepped back automatically and the sheriff droped a hand to his gun butt. 'Stand back from the bars, you!'

Although it hurt his swollen mouth, Adams smiled faintly.'You gonna come in here and make me, Sheriff?'

'I do, you'll know it! Well, what you think, Tess? This look or sound anythin' like the feller shot your pa?'

Adams pricked his ears up at that, watched the girl more closely. She seemed serious – well, it was a serious business, naturally – but she seemed to be taking great care not to make any mistakes, refusing to be hurried by Kendrick.

'Well, what you think, Tess?'

She waved a hand at the impatient sheriff, moved along the passage a little, had Adams walk away from

34

her across the cell, turn side-on. Finally, she looked back at Kendrick.

'All I can say with certainty, Nate, is that he looks to be about the right height. But he's thinner than the man I recall and I can't tell anything from the way he walks, because he's limping – from whatever injury he received since his arrest.' She paused but Kendrick made no comment. 'I'm afraid I can't testify to anything that would defintely identify him as the man who killed Dad – or was even a member of the gang of bank robbers.'

Kendrick was not pleased. 'Judas. Well, Tess, I thought with your pa bein' shot down in cold blood right beside you, you'd remember somethin' more definite than what you say!'

'I told you, Nate. Apart from the name and general build, I can not swear this man is my father's killer. And, believe me, I'd really like to do just that!'

'Well, he's got the right name: he's admitted that much. We found that hood at the bottom of his warbag, too. We'll have others who were in the bank at the time look at him. Don't worry: he'll be tried and hung, if he's guilty.'

They were walking away down the passage now and Adams returned slowly to the bunk, his body aching from the beating he had taken.

Things did not look good. Someone was setting him up and the shadow of the gallows was squarely upon him.

And just to top off a miserable day, the storm broke thirty minutes later, with torrential rain and high winds that blew the rain into the cell. Water streamed down two of the walls, splashed through the window on to his bunk so that he had to drag it into the middle of the cell. Lightning sizzled and crackled, thunder boomed. The roof leaked and no one brought him any supper.

It looked like a thoroughly miserable night ahead.

And it was – until he saw something moving at the barred window.

Something on the *outside*.

A big hat, a glistening slicker, an arm reaching through the bars and tossing something on to the bunk. Then whoever it was was gone and Adams stood up from where he was huddled in the only dry corner of the cell. Watching the barred window where lightning ripped through the night and rain splashed in like ricocheting bullets, he went to the sodden bunk, groped around in the flickering dark and found what had been tossed into his cell.

It was a Colt revolver – wet, and fully loaded.

CHAPTER 4

STORMY PASSAGE

It was still early in the night and from the window, pulling himself up by the bars, Adams could see a few lights still on in town. The general store, probably, certainly the saloons, and the livery.

'Dunno how many people might still be about despite the rain,' he muttered dropping back and fingering the Colt.

Someone wanted to help, anyway . . . Or did they? It could be a trap – the deputies said there was lynch talk in one of the saloons – could this be another way of making sure the man they figured had robbed and killed paid the penalty? Break out, only to run into a bullet. . . ?

It would sound good: shot and killed while trying to escape.

It was a possibility he had to face. But it came down to one thing: he had been given a chance and he would be crazy not to take it – no matter what the risk.

There would be no second chance – not in this town.

So he waited, sitting in his more-or-less dry corner nursing the gun. He pushed the loading gate aside, tipped out one of the shells, hefted it. It felt about right, fully loaded, not just an empty case with a lead slug pushed in to make him think it was a live cartridge.

There was one way to find out. He unloaded the gun, picked a shell at random and jammed the nose of the bullet in the muzzle, holding it firmly against the rifling in the end of the barrel. A quick twist and the slug came free of the brass case – and gunpowder spilled on to his fingers. He quickly held the case upright so as not to spill more than a few grains and then pushed the bullet back in.

So – they were live shells. Now, how did he use the gun to get out of here? The storm was still raging so he could yell his lungs out and no one would hear him and come running from the front office. *There must be some way . . .*

He waited impatiently, discarding wild plans until he eventually found one that would work. He lifted himself to the bars once more. There were only two lights burning now. One he guessed was a saloon, and the other he knew to be the livery, which likely stayed open all night.

The storm was easing, not much thunder and lightning now, but still plenty of rain. That would be in his favour – but first he had to get someone to open the door of his cell.

He tried yelling without result, then sat down in

the middle of the floor, ignoring the puddle from rain that had blown in, took the Colt and steadied it in both hands – and fired, so the bullet passed between the bars.The sound of the gun was easily distinguished from the low rumble of the dwindling thunderclaps.

Quickly he spread himself out on his face, the gun under his body, held firmly in his right hand.

He heard the office door slam open and the sounds of a man running towards the cell. Boots skidded to a stop and he heard a curse as lightning flashed and outlined his still, spread-eagled body lying in the puddle of rainwater.

'Christ! They did it!' The low voice was that of Renny Kendrick – and that suited Cole Adams just fine. As the key rattled in the lock and the door squeaked open on its hinges, Renny murmured again. 'They said they'd get the son of a bitch somehow, even if we stopped a lynch party. So they shot him through the window.' He was down on one knee now, reached for Adams's shoulder and heaved him on to his side.

Cole brought up the Colt and cocked the hammer with the muzzle, reeking of gunpowder, an inch from Kendrick's startled face. The man was so surprised he almost overbalanced. Cole lunged up and slammed him across the side of the head with the gun barrel, knocking off the man's hat. Even as Renny started to fall, Cole kicked him under the jaw, making sure he was well and truly out to it.

There was only one deputy on duty on a night like this so he took time to bind and gag Renny with the

39

man's own belt and clothing. He stuffed him under the bunk where rain still poured in, buckled on the man's gunrig, keeping the Colt that had been tossed through the window. He locked the cell door, took the keys with him and hurried down to the front office where an oil lamp on the desk burned with a low flame.

In minutes, he had his own hat, a slicker from a cupboard and a rifle from the gun cabinet, along with three boxes of ammunition. He propped a chair under the front-door handle so it would be more difficult to open from the outside and went out the back door, locking it behind him and breaking off the key, deliberately jamming the mechanism.

By the time they got Renny out of there it would be nearly high noon. . . .

Main Street was deserted, rain-lashed, signs creaking in the wind. He made his way to the livery and found Perry asleep in his small office, snoring in a tilted-back chair. He kicked the chair out from under the hostler and as the man sprawled, cursing and startled, lowered the rifle and prodded him in the chest.

'Judas priest!' Perry sat back, hands raised quickly. 'Take whatever you want – I ain't no hero.'

'Who went through my things beside Renny Kendrick?'

The livery man blinked and thought for a moment, shook his head. 'No one, far as I know.'

'Far as you know?'

'Well, my stablehand went home with a bellyache and I went down to the Gallant Gal, had me a coupla

40

beers – and a whiskey. Sort of – fortified myself because it was such a lousy night, you know—'

'So someone could've come in and planted that hood in my warbag?'

'We-ell – yeah, I guess so but – weren't too many folk movin' around in that storm, mister. Fact, I was gonna close early but musta dozed off.'

'Saddle my black and if you've got any grub on hand, give it to me. Pronto!'

The man had a half-eaten cold beefsteak pie which Adams wolfed down, then drank some cold coffee out of a half-filled tin mug, stuffed some crumbly biscuits into his slicker pockets.

Perry led the saddled black gelding down the aisle, looking very white and apprehensive. 'What – you gonna do with me?'

'Can't have you raising the alarm, can I?'

'Aw, Christ, I won't do that! Honest! Look, mister, I got me a wife and six kids, another on the way. I . . . they'd never make it without me! I work like a dog to keep 'em in grub an' clothes as it is, an'—'

'You're a fine upstanding citizen and a good husband. Friend, I'm sorry to have to do this.'

Adams clipped him across the back of the head with the rifle butt and the man sighed and collapsed at his feet. He bound and gagged him – there was plenty of rope available – and put him in an almost empty grain bin, propping the lid open a couple of inches with an old horseshoe so the man wouldn't suffocate.

Then he mounted the black, tugged down his hat and rode out into the wind-and-rain-lashed night.

Tess Fowler knew Indian Creek would be in flood after all the heavy rain.

She rose before daylight. The storm had blown itself out in the early hours but the air still felt damp and, when the sun came over the Saddleback, she knew it would be as hot and steamy as a Chinese laundry. Some of the hands were stirring in the bunkhouse and the cook already had his fires going when she rode out on her roan with the white-tipped ear.

She saw Jimmy Cross already riding along the trail to the creek pasture but by the time she caught him up he was sitting his horse on a low spur, hands resting on the saddle horn, staring at the racing, muddy waters.

'Must be a four-leaf clover growin' somewheres on Lazy F,' the foreman said without turning. 'Just look at that creek. One more foot, no, just another six inches, and it'd be over the bank, turnin' the pasture into a bog.'

Tess felt relief as the tension that had given her a sleepless night drained out of her. She smiled at the foreman who was about one-eighth Cherokee.

'Luck of the Irish, all right, Jim! You can bring the small herd down after breakfast. I don't think we're in for any more rain.'

His brown eyes rapidly scanned the blue sky to the horizon where just a few blotches of cotton wool hung over the ranges. 'No. We can risk it, Tess, but I'd like to give it till after noon, preferably tomorrow mornin'.'

'Why?'

A lean man with high cheekbones and prominent brows, he gestured to the creek. 'Cow wanders over too close to the water and the bank's sodden enough to give way under it . . .'

He didn't have to spell it out for her. She nodded. 'Whenever you think it's safe, Jim. And have Curly check the wire on those fences along the north-west line – at least one section is sagging.'

He touched a hand to his hatbrim, wheeled his mount and rode off. She watched the swift-flowing creek a little longer, rode upstream, but the usual ford was running at too fast a rate for her to risk crossing.

So she rode on to the Saddlebacks and put the roan up to the ridge her cowhands called Peacepipe, for no good reason that she could discover. It overlooked her land, sweeping away into the tangle of hills and canyons and for the hundredth time she vowed she would make time to take a crew of experienced cowhands in there and prepare some new pastures, clear some brush, fence them in. Her father had always said the grassy, waterfed canyons in there could be utilized if ever their herd grew large enough. They had never had to bother about them when he was alive, but now that she had a contract with the Boone & Davis meat agency, she was planning on expanding her herds, which meant that more safe pastures, with good water and grass, would be needed.

Looking around, enjoying the freshness of the air and the clean, washed look to the hills and vegetation, she suddenly straightened and stood in the stir-rups.

There was a rider down there, making his way cautiously along a narrow, muddy trail which she knew dropped down into a short pass. She suddenly drew in a sharp breath.

The man was riding a black horse and wearing a checked shirt. She squinted, shaded her eyes with her hand, to get a better look. *Yes!* She was sure of it now!

That was the same man Nate Kendrick had had in his jail, the one the sheriff claimed had murdered her father in cold blood – Cole Adams. Foolishly, she had been afraid to identify him in case she made a mistake.

He was moving furtively, stopping to look behind and up and down the slopes, rifle in hand all the time, obviously alert and on edge. Instinctively, she backed her roan behind a rock, dismounted and watched him through a gap between two boulders.

'Surely Nate Kendrick didn't let him go!' she said aloud, causing her horse to lift its head from a bunch of sweetgrass it was cropping.'No – the sheriff was positive this was the man they wanted . . . certainly "Cole Adams" was the name one of the hooded robbers had used during the bank robbery . . .' She remembered that very clearly.

And if Nate had let him go, it could mean only one thing!

She felt her heart start to race. She moved to the roan and slid her rifle from the saddle scabbard. She levered in a shell and returned to the gap

44

between the boulders, wondering if she had the courage to face down an escaped murderer who would no doubt be desperate and ruthless in his efforts to stay free.

But Cole Adams was sitting his black horse just this side of a bend in the trail, his hands raised and his rifle back in the saddle boot.

Someone she couldn't see because of a jutting rock was obviously holding a gun on Adams.

Well, if he had escaped, it looked like he had been recaptured now.

She was a little ashamed of the utter relief she felt now that she wouldn't have to face him alone.

The heavy rain accompanying the storm had worked in Adams's favour when he had cleared town. No ground could hold tracks in such a downpour and there was no one around to see which trail he took when he reached the edge of town.

He didn't know this country, had come into Gallant from the other side, but he recalled seeing a range of hills to the north so he rode in that general direction. The drumming of the rain on his slicker and stiff hatbrim irritated him. He hadn't been used to such luxuries for years: when he was prospecting, if it rained hard, he simply moved into his tunnel and worked there till it stopped.

He came to a creek that was raging with brown, frothing water, carrying small saplings and branches past at eye-blurring speed. He rode upstream and down but found nowhere safe to cross, so headed up into the foothills. The rain was easing now and he saw that the creek swung away here to flow across what looked like ranch land.

He didn't want to be seen so rode deeper into the hills, twice having to dismount and lead the protesting black over washaways on the narrow trail. There was a tolerably dry spot beneath an overhang of rock and he decided to stop there: no sense in risking riding off the edge of a sodden trail in the dark.

He dozed, rifle across his thighs, and was surprised when he opened his eyes and saw the grey light of a beginning day. The rain had stopped and a few white clouds scudded across a mostly blue sky. He was glad to shrug off the slicker but tied it behind the cantle. It had kept him mostly dry. He was hungry and ate the crumbly biscuits he had taken from the livery. They were stale and turned to a tasteless paste in his mouth but had to suffice. He wanted hot coffee and a cigarette but had neither, drank rainwater from a depression in a rock just outside his shelter.

The black seemed eager to move on and he mounted, riding warily, holding his rifle with a shell in the breech.

Steam began to rise from the ground and he saw a few cattle browsing on the wet grass on a hillside pasture. He rode close enough to a section of fence with sagging wire to read the brand on the hip of one steer: a slanting 'F' above a horizontal line. *Lazy F.*

He rode away from the fence line, the trail angling down a little now. He could hear the roar of the creek's floodwaters and turned away over a small rise, came down to a winding trail that crossed a low spur.

He kept that spur between himself and the ranch

pastures; some cowhands would likely be out early, checking for storm damage, and the fewer folk who saw him the better.

Then he started to round a bend where a large pointed boulder leaned outwards, forcing him to the very edge of the trail. Cole Adams was concentrating on this, making sure it was safe enough for the horse to walk on, when he heard the lever of a rifle working – just a few feet away.

There were three men blocking the trail around the leaning rock. Two had rifles, the third held a cocked sixgun. They didn't have to tell him to sheath his rifle or raise his hands. He did both, watching these strangers warily.

'Kendrick got a posse out a damn sight faster then I figured,' he said with quiet bitterness.

The men exchanged amused glances and the one with the sixgun, black-bearded and wall-eyed, chuckled out loud.

'Hell, man, you ain't that lucky! We're not part of no posse. But you sure as hell will wish we were before we're finished with you!'

CHAPTER 5

GHOST

Sheriff Nate Kendrick was so mad he could barely speak. Renny Kendrick, nursing a sore head, took a polished steel mirror from his shirt pocket, examined the cut from the gunwhipping, then patted his hair back into place.

'Forget your damn hair! You're hopeless, boy!'

'He must've fired the gun himself, then lain down in the pool of water, Pa. I thought someone had shot him through the window.'

'Where the hell did he get the gun?' snarled the sheriff, glaring at his son. 'Didn't you smell gunsmoke when you walked into the cell?'

'I – I guess I did – but I thought it was from someone shootin' through the bars.'

'You guess! Hell almighty, boy, you guessed *wrong*! And now the son of a bitch is gone – and we won't find a single track after all that goddamn rain.'

Renny lifted his head slowly, tried to sound

encouraging. 'Rain's stopped now, Pa. Ground'll be muddy and it'll hold tracks as it dries. With no rain to wash 'em out, they'll stand out like dogs' balls.' He pocketed the mirror.

'You think so, eh? And just where the hell do we look for these tracks that're gonna lead us to the most important prisoner we ever had in the cells – *and lost?*'

Renny made a vague gesture. 'We'll whip up a big posse, Pa. Make the sons of bitches ride with us, scatter 'em all round the countryside, clear out to the ranges. We're bound to cut his trail.'

Nate grunted, grudgingly admitted it was on a bigger scale than he had ever handled but it just might work.

'Why you reckon Adams is so important, Pa? We got dodgers on outlaws with bigger bounties on 'em than him.'

Nate Kendrick made a savage gesture, knocking over his coffee-tin humidor and cursing as tobacco spilled over the papers on his desk.

'Bounties don't count here – we won't see nothin' more'n a 'thank you', mebbe a bottle of bourbon or somethin'. But this feller's scared the pants of everyone in three states! He's robbed and killed. We bring him to trial and we're gonna be famous. *Harper's* an' Eastern papers'll send someone to cover the trial. *Local Lawmen Capture Bloody-Handed Killer!* We'll make big names for ourselves and we'll attract a lot more money than the damn reward. Sell our story, public appearances . . . Travel, with all expenses paid, boy!'

49

Renny nodded slowly, smiled. 'Hey! I never thought of that! Hell, Pa, that's – that's right smart thinkin'!'

'Yeah! Now all we gotta do is find Cole Adams. I oughta kick your butt for you, Renny, big an' all as you are, lettin' him get away!'

'Judas, I never let him getaway! He'd still be in his cell if someone hadn't tossed him a gun! If we could find out who done that—'

'It'd take us from now till next Christmas! No – you start gettin' a posse together. I'll go tear a strip off Andy Perry so's he'll feel bad an' supply spare hosses free of charge.'

So the Kendricks got their posse together, a large one, over twenty men. Nate took charge and scattered them in groups of three to search around for tracks; the signal, if they found anything promising, was to be three shots, a break, then a fourth shot.

No one seemed particularly enthusiastic but they knew their sheriff: when Nate Kendrick fell into one of his black moods, folk had better listen and do what Kendrick wanted – or they'd find they'd broken some obscure law they'd never heard of and would languish in jail until Nate returned with his posse.

Even though they knew what kind of tracks Adams's mount made after studying those left by the black in Perry's livery, there was no success. Several false alarms brought posse men riding in from all points of the compass in answer to the prearranged signal, but always something was not quite right or the tracks led nowhere, petered out.

'We ain't never gonna find his trail this way, Nate,'

growled one of the townsmen. It was almost noon now and the sun was drying out the ground fast. The rain had been so heavy that it had blurred or washed out most sign, and there were few tracks that could be said definitely to have been made since the rain stopped.

'We'll find him!' snapped the sheriff. 'Spread out and keep lookin'.'

'Why not head straight for the hills, Pa?' suggested Renny, his head still throbbing. 'I reckon he'd make for there – only place he could hide really. Too much open country, else.'

The deputy was surprised when his father agreed almost immediately. 'Been thinkin' along those lines. But we'll split again. This time into two. Renny, you take half the men and follow the river. He might've tried to get back over the state line. I'll take the rest of the boys up into the Saddlebacks. We'll rendezvous at the Anvil swing-station at sundown, unless we're lucky before that and nail the bastard.'

With empty bellies growling for food and coffee, they split up and rode off in their separate directions, grim-faced and mean-eyed.

Nate Kendrick knew he would have to watch that someone didn't put a bullet into Adams if he was spotted. He wanted that court case – with his name in the newspapers as the man who had brought this killer to justice.

He had been a frontier lawman for twenty years. It was about time he enjoyed some real fame – and Cole Adams was the man who was going to get it for him.

*

51

Adams kept looking at the man with brown hair. He had not long shaved – or been shaved – and the hair had a freshly cut look to it. The sides of his face and upper lip were pale against the walnut skin of cheeks and nose.

'The hell you keep lookin' at me for?' the man growled as they climbed one of the steep slopes of the Saddlebacks. The bearded man with the wall eye led the way, followed by a squat man who hadn't yet spoken. Adams rode with hands tied to the saddle horn, holster empty, the sixgun someone had tossed into the cell also taken. The man with the short hair and newly shaven face rode alongside, though slightly to the rear.

Adams turned his head slightly at the man's question. 'Believe I bought you a drink in the Gallant saloon.'

The man grinned. 'Taken you all this time to recognize me, eh?' He scrubbed a hand around his smooth jowls. 'Good barber that feller. Surprised you didn't recognize me earlier – but you were talkin' to that red-haired *hombre* when I left the barbershop.' He patted the sixgun rammed into the belt, the one he had taken from Adams not long ago. 'Good to have my own gun back.'

Cole started. 'You tossed that gun into my cell? Why?'

'Got you out, didn't it? 'Course, we thought you might shoot someone durin' the breakout, rile everyone up – and they'd lift the reward a few more hundred.'

The prisoner frowned, digesting that as the man

52

smirked. The bearded rider called back, 'Whyn't you shut up, Taft?'

'Why don't you? You're paid to be the pathfinder, an' nothin' else, Crewe.'

'I don't know you,' Adams said to Taft. 'Why would you help me? Then grab me and tie me up again?'

Taft said nothing but Adams nodded slowly. 'You mentioned a reward. Guess there's one on my head I dunno about?'

Taft and the squat man laughed. 'You hear that, Crewe? He wants to know if there's a re-ward for him?'

"Well, I guess you'll tell him."

Taft snorted, leaned from the saddle and punched Adams's shoulder. 'Mister, the name of Cole Adams has got the folk of three states so riled up that they've put a bounty on you that totals up to nigh on twelve thousand dollars!'

Adams went cold. God! What the hell was he supposed to've done to have a bounty that big riding on him?

The trio thought it was right funny the way he looked in his state of shock, even Crewe twisting his hairy mouth into some kind of grin.

Cole started to speak, then changed his mind. That's what they wanted! They were baiting him so he'd ask a lot of stupid questions and they'd give him stupid answers so that he'd learn nothing . . . Better to try and figure something out himself. . . . And that wouldn't be easy!

There was so little to go on: he wrote his name in that assay book in Gallant and the damn sky fell in on

53

him. There was talk of stage hold-ups, bank robberies, Wells Fargo Express office thefts – and the killing of witnesses.

And the dropping of his name on several occasions!

That was where the trouble lay: his name had been mentioned at some of those crimes, deliberately; though it seemed that each time 'he' or someone pretending to be Cole Adams, had berated the outlaw who had spoken his name. Everyone was hooded so no features could be seen, not even hair colour. Which was why there were no pictures on the wanted dodgers, only varying descriptions that matched on several details: just over six feet, rangy build, but good shoulders, long arms and legs, seemed to favour checked shirts, voice muffled by the flour-sack hood but generally described as 'deep' – one woman passenger said it was 'wonderfully manly', whatever the hell that meant – and others couldn't make up their minds how it sounded.

But none of that mattered: *it was his name that everyone remembered hearing at the scenes of the crimes.*

It told him the obvious: someone was deliberately framing him for all these thefts and killings.

But when he'd been caught and thrown into jail 'they' – or someone maybe not even connected with 'them' – broke him out.

What in the hell was going on?

As if Taft had read his mind, the man, still highly amused, said, 'Won't be long and you'll find out. Thought we'd lost track of you for a spell, but then you turned up in Redwood and paid for your provisions with gold dust. Someone followed you to see where you got the gold.'

'Three men tried to jump my claim, but I killed them in a shoot-out.'

Taft, grinning, shook his head. 'Four – there was a fourth man. Got lost in all them twists and turns you made, arrived just as you finished off the others and he hid. After you left he scouted your camp, found a letter and miner's licence with 'C. Adams' on 'em. Had enough sense to bring 'em to us – didn' you, Crewe?'

Adams snapped his head up as the bearded man looked back soberly. 'My brother was one of them three you killed, you son of a bitch.'

'You're lucky I never saw you.'

Crewe started to swing his mount around but Taft held up his hand. 'Keep it for later – we're behind time as it is. Best keep goin'.'

They kept climbing and by dark were on the top of the range where they made a cold camp for the night. Adams was bound hand and foot, laid between two boulders and a heavy, flat slab of rock was pushed across the tops of them.

'Hey! I read someplace where the old Egyptians used to bury their kings in stone coffins,' said Taft. 'How is it, Adams? You feel like a mummy?'

The trio laughed and Cole had to fight to keep from struggling. The space was little bigger than a stone sarcophagus; he felt a rising panic but tried to put it from his mind. There was plenty of air. The slab couldn't fall on him. It was mighty uncomfortable but he could handle that. . . .

But he spent one hell of a night, slept hardly at all, and was more pleased than he thought possible when they uncovered him and untied him so he could relieve his bladder.

They allowed him to eat, the squat man, Punkin, cooking sowbelly and beans which tasted mighty good to Adams, despite all the stale grease and fat running over his chin.

Their trail went up and over, and before leaving Taft climbed a high rock and used field glasses to scan the country they had passed through yesterday and ahead to where they would be going today.

'They've got a posse out,' he reported when he climbed down. 'A big one. Saw two groups, one way back by the river, just in case he runs for the state line, I guess, other skirtin' that Fowler ranch, Lazy F. They won't find our tracks – or if they do, we'll be long gone.'

'Where?' Cole figured he had nothing to lose by asking and was surprised when Taft said,

'Not all that far – but in a place no one knows about except us. Hidden better'n that valley where you worked the gold.'

Adams said nothing but on the downtrail, riding alongside him, Taft asked, 'You leave much gold in that valley? Crewe said it looked like you'd caved in a tunnel.'

'Just managed to get out in time,' Cole lied. 'I'd found a few nuggets, was hoping to hit a mother lode or a big vein, when it caved in I figured that was a warning. Wasn't much more alluvial stuff left in the creek anyway, so I packed up and moved out.'

'Leavin' some tools and a tent and rockin'-cradle behind,' Taft said, looking sceptical. 'Sounds to me like you was plannin' on goin' back.'

Adams shrugged. 'Might've. I couldn't lug all that stuff out with me. One of my pack mules died – diamondback got him – and I'd built the cradle and tentframe on the spot, so just left 'em. If anyone finds the valley and wants to try their luck, they're welcome to 'em.'

Taft continued to study Adams's face: he still wasn't sure.

But if he was really interested in any gold that might still be there – well, it was something to remember.

Before sundown, he saw signs of a camp on a high ridge. There was a guard amongst some rocks who challenged them but Taft was soon recognized and they passed through a narrow, twisting path between huge boulders which led into a clearing, fringed with trees and brush, about two thirds of the way up the high mountain.

It looked like a permanent hideout, a couple of rough cabins, a rudimentary shelter for the horses, corrals, a small cascade of permanent water that trickled down a sandstone rockface into a small pool. Saddles and bedrolls lay scattered about; there were even some faded and worn clothes that had been strung out to dry on a rope line.

He counted six men lounging about. No one moved much, just cast a curious glance in his direction. Then the door of the highest cabin opened and a man stood there.

Tall as Adams but beefier, shirt strained over the wide shoulders. He carried one gun, holstered on the left side. He wore a glove on his right hand and tugged the fingers down firmly as he started towards the new arrivals. He limped slightly, favouring his left leg. His clothes were worn and faded, and then Cole looked at his face.

It was a brutal face, thick-lipped, jutting brows, scarred under his right eye: the nose had been hammered and spread considerably. He wore a tobacco-stained moustache, not too heavy, dark like his hair.

His eyes were some dark shade and were narrowed now as he walked up to Adams who still sat his black mount, bound wrists in his lap.

'Well, howdy-do, Cole Adams. Been a long time since Laramie.'

The man grabbed Adams's leg and heaved, throwing him out of the saddle. Cole landed hard with a grunt, and the big man stepped around the skittish black, cuffing it out of the way, walked up and drove a boot into Cole's side.

He leaned down over the grimacing prisoner.

'What's the matter? Don't recognize me? You look like you've seen a ghost!'

And that was how Cole Adams felt: he had believed this man – Leith Taylor – had died in a territorial prison, three years ago, while serving a ten-year stretch for his attack on Adams's wife that led to her death.

CHAPTER 6

THE OUTLAW

It happened five years ago, and he had almost, but not quite, put it behind him. Now . . .

Cole Adams and his new bride, Barbara, had moved into their log cabin which they had built between them, living in a tent while doing it. He levelled the earthen floor and she, more artistically inclined than her husband, made intricate designs in the packed earth. Swept clean and filled with small pieces of pale gravel and sand from the nearby stream, it made an unusual and attractive floor.

Adams made the furniture as the weeks moved along towards fall and he cut and split plenty of pine logs for when winter arrived. It would be icy in this open country.

They were a little ahead of schedule on their prove-up time and once the cabin was habitable, a well dug and operating to save the walk to the stream, he began taking temporary work on nearby ranches. The money went towards buying a small herd of cattle and he spent time making a split-rail fence around the best pasture, which happened to be furthest from the cabin. It was back-breaking work for a man alone and Barbara made a habit of taking him his lunch so he wouldn't have to make the long walk back to the cabin. By this time she was several months pregnant and he told her to forget about the lunch.

'I can work through without it. Two meals a day is fine with me.'

'But you use so much energy working, Cole – you need to have the extra food.'

They compromised by arranging to meet by a bend of the stream, where they would sit and eat lunch together, sometimes just drinking stream water, at others, lemonade, even hot coffee which she brewed and brought in a clay jug.

They were happy times and he often wondered what he had ever done to deserve a beautiful wife like Barbara and such a wonderful section of Wyoming in which to build their home.

Then on a crisp fall day, the big sky blue and cloudless from horizon to horizon, the yellow-red leaves adding extra colour to the forest, it all changed.

Leith Taylor rode in on a stolen horse, half-starved, a bullet wound across his back under his right shoulder.

Barbara, her golden hair freshly washed and shining in the bright sun, was at the well, just setting the wooden pail on the stone edge, when the rider appeared around the side of the cabin. He startled her for she hadn't heard the horse approach and when she saw his unshaven and dishevelled appearance, she felt a coldness grip her heart.

Here was a man on the run if ever she saw one – and there had been a few passing through. Most were content to have a meal and move on, though there had been two who had tried to take fresh horses. Cole had shot one and driven the other off. But this man she *knew* right away was not going to merely refresh himself and pass on through.

He grinned through the dirt-clogged stubble as he dismounted stiffly. Some women would think him good-looking, she thought as she saw the dried blood on the back of his torn shirt. The wound didn't seem to be bothering him unduly. He gestured to the pail of water.

'Could empty that at one draught, ma'am.'

Hand shaking, Barbara took the dipper that hung on a short chain on the upright of the winch. 'You're welcome to a drink. Your horse, too.'

He walked across and she could smell the wild trails on him: woodsmoke and, maybe, gunsmoke, stale sweat, horse . . . He took the dipper, allowing his hand to touch hers as he took it, smiled again as he scooped it full of well water. He drank three dipperfuls, one after the other.

'Better'n mother's milk.'

She frowned. 'Your horse. . . ?'

He glanced at the lathered, trail-battered paint whose head was hanging low. 'I'll swap him for one of yours. That grey in the corral looks like he could carry me far.'

61

'No!' she said firmly, heart racing but trying to look determined. 'You're welcome to let him drink, groom him if you want and get some of the filth off him. I'll give you some grain to take with you. But no swap.'

He pushed back his hat and scratched his scalp through the sweat-matted dark-brown hair, still grinning. *He knows he has a certain charm with women!* 'Now that ain't none too friendly, ma'am. Mebbe I should deal with your man . . .'

That was when the real fear gripped her. He looked around, smirking now. The barn had no doors on it yet and he could see it was empty. There was nowhere else anyone could be – except in the cabin.

'He's in the cabin,' she told him breathlessly, starting to move away from the well. 'I'll fetch him and you can talk with him about swapping your horse . . .'

She could see he knew she was lying but he shrugged and stood aside to let her move towards the cabin. She tried not to hurry and called,

'Cole – Cole! Can you spare a few minutes to talk with this man?'

Then she heard him laugh and she spun around. *He was only a few steps behind her!* Abandoning all pretence now, she hitched up her skirts and began to run for the cabin. There was a rifle above the door inside that Cole always insisted they keep there, loaded. He had shown her how to use it and she was a good shot. If she could only get to it . . .

But she knew she wasn't going to make it. A hand like a vice gripped one shoulder, spun her around and then his arms were crushing her against his foul-smelling body.

Cole Adams cursed as the large splinter drove deep into the palm of his left hand. It broke off, leaving a jagged edge. He tried several times to grab this to pull it out but it was soft wood, almost half an inch wide, and thick. And it had gone deep. Blood made it slippery. He tried using his teeth but the jagged ends only served to cut his lips.

Swearing, he tried to keep using the log splitter but the hickory handle passed right across the splinter and served only to drive it in further. He tried switching his stroke to the other side but when the splitter's blade twisted out of control and almost cut his leg he threw it down in a fit of temper and started walking back to the cabin. There was no other choice: he would just have to lose the time, have Barb remove the goddamn splinter and bandage the hand.

He would carry the scar for the rest of his life – as if he needed reminding about what happened this terrible day . . .

He was sweating by the time he topped the small rise that stood between the cabin and the field where he had been working, and he rested against a tree to get his breath.

As soon as he saw the jaded paint horse standing by the corral he tensed. A quick glance showed him no sign of Barbara or the rider of the paint. His gaze went to the cabin.

The door stood half-open. The rocker he had made for Barbara lay on its side on the small porch. One of her shoes was at the foot of the two steps . . .

Then he was running, all kinds of wild thoughts flooding through his mind, terrifying him. He was not conscious of clenching his fists, unfeeling of the big splinter deep in the palm of his left hand. He had no weapons: this was a peaceful valley and he had never even worn a gun rig or taken a rifle with him when he worked away from the house. After all, he was only a quarter-mile away ... And this day he found out just how long that quarter-mile could be.

'*Barbara! Barbara!*'

He yelled as he approached and leapt up the steps, just as a big man appeared in the doorway, sixgun in hand. His stubbled face was scratched and bleeding, his shirt hung in tatters from his waistband, and even in that blurred glimpse, Adams saw Barbara's teeth-marks on the man's torso, where she had tried desperately to fight him off.

The gun came up and Cole snatched the rocking-chair by the back, swung it violently. The Colt roared and the chair splintered against the doorframe. But Cole held on to the remains, thrust forward, his whole weight behind it. Leith Taylor retreated because he had no choice: it was like being run over by a train.

He tripped and went down and Adams smashed the chair's remains across his head, stomped cruelly on the gun hand, bones crunching. The weapon skidded away and Taylor yelled in pain. Even while he kicked the man's ribs in, Cole shouted for Barbara, then glimpsed her lying on the floor by the bed. The blanket screen had been torn from its cord, lay in a heap, partly across one of her bruised legs.

She was half-naked and the sight of her swollen body drove him into a frenzy.

He pulled Taylor up by the hair, smashed him in the face with countless hammer blows from his fist, feeling the nose crunch and spread, blood spurting, teeth breaking. He felt no pain from the big splinter in his left hand although his blood mixed with Taylor's now. He flung the man against the wall, and Taylor's head crashed into the logs. His legs began to fold and Cole stood back, took deliberate aim and kicked the man in the groin. He didn't allow Taylor to fall, but hurled him completely across the room. He fell, skidding down the log wall into a sitting position, unconscious, gun hand a mess of protruding bones and torn, bloody flesh.

Tears blinding him, Adams gave Taylor one more kick and ran to Barbara. She was conscious, almost choked him as her arms went around his neck, crushing herself to him, sobbing his name over and over.

He didn't know how long he held her that way, but she cried until all that was left was a dry half-cough, half-choking sound, shaking her entire abused body.

Horses came into the yard and a man appeared in the doorway, holding a gun.

'Cole? You all right. Oh, Jesus! Missus OK. . . ?'

It was Sheriff Nolan from Laramie. He had led in the posse that was on the trail of Leith Taylor, an outlaw wanted for several robberies, some with violence, one with rape. Maybe two, now . . .

Adams rigged the blanket and helped Barbara clean up but she was doubled over with knifing pains in the abdomen, blood trickling down her inner thighs.

'Best get her to a doctor,' Nolan advised, watching his men carry the manacled and still unconscious Taylor outside. 'Thing is, Doc Salmon was in an all-night poker game with Lew Gannon from the Double C. Doc won and – well, he's been celebratin', drunk as I've ever seen him, Cole. Likely out to it by now. He won't be much help, I'm afraid.'

'Goddamn him!' Cole gritted. 'That means I'll have to take her to Cheyenne!'

Nolan, a middle-aged family man, nodded and said quietly, looking at Barbara, 'I – wouldn't waste too much time, Cole. I'll send one of the posse on ahead and mebbe a doctor can meet you out along the trail.'

That was the best on offer. But it wasn't good enough. They hadn't travelled fifteen miles in the shaky buckboard, Barbara trying not to cry out with the pain, the bleeding getting worse, when the rear wheel collapsed and the vehicle overturned, rolling down a steep bank into the river. Cole was the only survivor – even the horses had been killed – and there were many times since when he wished he had been, too.

He should have killed Leith Taylor – almost had, and the man's lawyer at his trial made much of it.

'Excessive and extreme force, Judge! Mr Taylor never even had a chance to explain how he found Mrs Adams lying there, already injured, when he arrived—'

'And how does he explain the condition he was in?' the judge interrupted angrily. 'Scratched and bitten . . .'

66

'That was never actually established, Judge. You know my client's injuries were too extensive to be certain of those claims by – er – Mr Adams. The man attacked my client and brutally beat him and while Mr Taylor may be guilty of other crimes, he has a right to justice the same as—'

The judge said coldly: 'I believe I would have done exactly the same thing as Mr Adams.'

'Judge, we're not disputing the guilty verdict right now – though there will be an appeal, I give you fair notice – but whether a man like Adams should be allowed to roam free. I mean, what is the risk to the general public? I believe he has already been involved in a drunken brawl in one saloon. "Drowning his sorrows" someone said in his defence!'

The judge signed resignedly. 'Very well, Mr Iles. I see your point and I want it on record that I will not hear any case in my court where you are employed as legal counsel ever again. You will be satisfied if I sentence Mr Adams for use of "excessive force" as you call it upon your client?'

Iles smiled coldly. 'Whatever you decide, Judge.'

'Good. Cole Adams, I sentence you to three weeks work on the chaingang now building the new north-west road outside of Cheyenne.' The gavel banged loudly. 'Sit *down*, Mr Iles! I have made my ruling.' He turned to Cole Adams who sat as if in a dream, unaware and uncaring of events going on around him.

'Sentence can be served when you have time to leave your own work, Mr Adams,' the judge added, to the fury of Taylor's lawyer. 'The court understands that because of delays in this trial and' – he glared at Iles – 'for other reasons, you are now running against the clock to prove-up on time . . .'

But with Barbara dead, Cole had no interest in the ranch they had planned to build; he had little interest in *anything*. The bottom had dropped out of his world.

After the chaingang, he rode away, leaving the land just as it was, except that he burned the cabin and barn to the ground. He stayed in Cheyenne just long enough to see Leith Taylor sentenced to a minimum of ten years on the rockpile. As the barred prison wagon rolled by, Taylor, still battered and bandaged, clung to the ironwork and glared at Adams sitting on his horse, watching soberly.

'I'll be out some day, sodbuster!'

'And I'll be waiting,' Cole said, meaning it at the time.

But, of course, it faded with the years. He consoled himself with the thought of how Taylor was rotting in prison. And there was one more thing: there had been a $700 reward for Taylor's capture and Sheriff Nolan made sure it was paid to Cole Adams. He stared at the money as if he didn't know what to do with it. There were all kinds of advice about investing in more land and cattle, but in the end, over a period of six months, he spent the lot. His way.

Mostly it went on booze, almost killing him, until some backwoods doctor took him in hand, made him feel ashamed by asking him to think honestly about what his dead wife would say if she could see him now. It sobered him more than anything else, and that wise old sawbones nursed him back to health and turned his thinking around.

When word came through that Leith Taylor had been killed in prison in a knife fight, that seemed to be a good omen to Cole Adams: it was like the closing off of a terrible part of his life. He decided to do his best to put it behind him and start anew.

For a couple of years he led the life of a drifting cowpoke, following the cattle trails up and down the country. Then one winter he found an old prospector with a couple of Sioux arrows in him and nursed the man through. The old man in gratitude taught him how to prospect for gold and told him about a secret valley he knew of that contained a mighty rich vein of almost pure gold.

'It ain't the ramblin's of some old sourdough nigh off his head from too much dreamin'. This is real, son, but I'm just too old and weak to work it. But you can do it.'

'How about we work it together?'

The old man smiled, showing his toothless gums. 'Like nothin' better, Cole, but – well, the old ticker ain't so good and . . . I been feelin' strange these past few days. Left shoulder and arm tinglin', chest feelin' like a hoss is standin' on it, short of breath. I know the signs. I reckon I'll have to pass—'

'We'll get you to a sawbones and see what—'

'Don't think I'll make it, son. I've had two of these before and they told me the next one'd be the last.'

The old man was right. He was dead in a week and Cole buried him in an unmarked grave. He went into the nearest town, drank a silent toast to the old prospector's memory and rode out, following the old man's directions to the valley where riches lay waiting to be gathered.

The mother lode that the old prospector had told him about had eluded him, was still there – maybe. One day he might go back and open up that tunnel again.

That had been his plan, anyway, when he had ridden into Gallant. Spend the little bit of gold he had found, have a break from the monotony of digging or washing gravel, day after day; then, refreshed, start work again on the tunnel. But now the past had caught up with him and Leith Taylor was back, ready and eager to claim his pound of flesh.

CHAPTER 7

REVENGE

Leith Taylor walked up from the campfire, chewing on a leg of some kind of wildfowl Crewe had shot earlier. He spat a piece of tough skin into his prisoner's lap.

Cole Adams was bound hand and foot but there was a sapling across his shoulders like a yoke, one hand bound to each end, arms stretched. His feet were crossed and tied very tightly so that he could no longer feel his toes. Already there was fresh blood at his nostrils and dripping from his chin. One eye was swollen and half-closed.

'You know, I used to be thought a fair-looking man one time,' Taylor said around a mouthful of stringy meat. 'Not handsome or one of them pretty boys you see in the medicine shows or on the stage, but not bad. Women seemed to like the way I looked, anyway.'

He suddenly spat the half-chewed meat into

Adams's face. 'Then I rode into that damn quarter-section of yours. Look at me now! Nose is smashed up; "crushed and deviated septum" the butcher they called a doctor in prison told me. Stuffed about five yards of bandage up there after scrapin' and drillin'. Judas, just thinking about it makes my eyes water! Sight ain't what it used to be in my left eye, neither.' He kicked Cole in the already bruised ribs.

Adams managed to pull his knees up a little, an instinctive move, to help ease the pain, but it still hurt like hell. Taylor glared down at him, his left hand opening and closing. The right hand was still covered by a dark chamois glove. He held it up now.

'You not only ruined what looks I had, you busted my gun hand! Never was any good after you stomped on it!'

'Should've done the same to your face and made a really good job of it,' slurred Adams.

'Aaaaagh!' Taylor growled, reached down, yanked Cole's hair and slammed his head back against the boulder behind him. 'By the time I'm finished with you, no one'll recognize you. Oops! No, I gotta remember to leave enough of you for the marshals to be sure it's you – before they hand over the re-ward.'

Adams frowned, looking up at the man's dimly seen face, the firelight flickering behind him. He arched his eyebrows at Adams, urging, looking expectant, and Cole realized that the man was waiting for him to say something – *no, not just say something – he was waiting for Cole to acknowledge that he understood what was being said!*

And suddenly he saw it, his battered mouth

72

sagging open in disbelief.

'You – you're gonna beat the hell outta me, likely kill me – then – collect the bounty! This is your revenge?'

Leith Taylor grinned, spreading his hands. 'Now, if I had a cee-gar, Adams, I'd give you one, I really would. I might even untie you and let you smoke it. That was right smart thinking, working that out.'

'It's plumb loco! You wouldn't dare show your face, even to collect twelve thousand bucks – or however much it is.'

'Just shy of fifteen thousand right now. See, there was this town with two banks and you – or someone using your name – held 'em up, with a gang that was mighty quick on the trigger. Couple folk got killed, they tell me – one a woman bank clerk. Ricocheting bullet, but she still died durin' the hold-up, so counts as murder.'

'You son of a bitch! You've dropped my name all over three states! I'm lucky Nate Kendrick or Renny didn't shoot me on sight!'

Taylor turned and grinned at the rest of his gang as they sat around, smoking, eating, drinking the powerful coffee, and listening to him talk with the prisoner.

'Yeah, you are a real bad-ass, Cole. All them naughty things you done. *Tut-tut*! An' each time someone "accidentally" called you by name, the reward went up another hundred bucks or more.'

Taylor paused and after a while Cole Adams shook his head.

'I don't believe it! You did all these things I'm being blamed for – murder, robbery, and hell knows what else – just to build up a big bounty on me? That's – crazy!'

Taylor smiled crookedly and scratched at one ear, then rolled a cigarette and lit up before answering.

'Mebbe – but look who's all tied up, an' worth nigh on fifteen thousand bucks – and look who's just waitin' to go and collect. You sure I'm the one that's crazy?'

Adams didn't say so out loud, but – Taylor had a point!

'See, you collected a bounty on me, didn't you? Aw, I know, just a piddlin' few hundred bucks, but that's what gave me the idea when I decided to bust out of the territorial prison and kill the son of a bitch that put me there. I used to dream every night about you, what I'd do to you, and what I wished I'd had time to do to your wife. What would the brat've been if it'd lived? Boy or gal?'

Adams's face became suffused with blood and he bared his teeth, struggling against the cruel bite of the ropes around his wrists and ankles. Pain seared across his shoulders. Taylor smirked, hunkering down now in front of Adams, but out of range of any kick that might come his way.

'Thought when I got out, I'd tell you in detail just what I done to your wife before you come in and smashed me up.' He laughed. 'Hey! You like that idea? Hell, I got the time – and you sure ain't goin' no place . . . Look, it was this way, once I got her into the cabin . . .'

Cole tried to close his ears and mind to the filth and horrific clinical details Taylor related. He was making animal sounds in his throat as some of the words reached his brain and felt he was going to throw up, writhed and twisted until blood ran from under the rope bonds.

The outlaws listened avidly, some asking Taylor to explain more fully. Adams, his face a mask of horror, looked at them one by one, remembering their features and names.

They were all dead men – once he got free!

Which seemed an impossibility right now, but as long as he was still breathing, he would keep trying: he'd find some way, even if it was only just long enough for a chance to kill Taylor.

He realized suddenly, through the buzzings and whistlings inside his head, that the outlaw leader had stopped speaking now. Cole looked at him with hooded, murderous eyes, and asked, 'How'd you – escape prison?'

Taylor grinned. 'Easier than anyone might think – There was a knife fight, all right. I won, though. I wasn't the feller they sewed up in a sack and dumped in the cellar till the next wagon was due to go to town and take along any bodies for burial – or to be cut up by the damn local doctor. With a few bribes – and a little help along the way – I changed places with the fool I'd knifed. He was found in my bunk next mornin', his face – well sorta hard to identify. The warders, who don't give a damn anyway, figured it must've been some friends of the dead man takin' their revenge . . . on me! It weren't hard once we reached town to cut my way outta the sack.'

Cole could tell Taylor was proud of his effort,

looked around at his men for their admiration. They gave it to him, but when Adams made no comment, Taylor kicked him hard in the thigh muscles and tossed the dregs of his coffee in his face.

'Took quite a while to track you down. Then I got the notion of droppin' your name when we pulled a job, all hooded-up so no one could identify us. But they'd remember your name! Then you made it easy by signing that assay book. Was gonna shoot you through the bars but that would've wasted all that bounty sittin' on your head. So, then I figured all I had to do was help you break out – and wait. There's nowhere else for a man on the run to hide around here except in these hills. We spread out and I knew sooner or later we'd run into you. Or, as it happened, you'd run into us.'

'I could've been shot trying to escape.'

Taylor shrugged. 'A risk I was prepared to take.' He grinned tightly. 'I mean, it wasn't my life I was gambling with, was it?'

'Well, I'll tell you something, Taylor. You better make a damn good job of whatever you've got planned for me. Because, if you don't, I'll get loose somehow – and you and every one of the scum who run with you will be dead within an hour!'

That brought some curses and catcalls and Leith Taylor casually kicked Adams in the chest, flicking his cigarette butt into the man's battered face.

'Keep dreamin', Adams. But sleep well – 'cause you got a long, busy day tomorrow.' He started to walk away, then paused, glanced over his shoulder and said casually, 'Payback starts at sun-up!'

*

The gang had booze with them, two bottles of some rotgut and a stone jug, likely moonshine purchased or stolen locally. It would probably eat its way through cast iron.

There was a lot of ribald laughter when Taylor repeated his story of how he had mistreated Barbara Adams five years ago. He kept looking over his shoulder at Adams, but Cole had let his head sag forward – although it hurt like hell, pulling on nerves already over-stretched by the sapling yoke – and pretended to be asleep or passed out.

Once they threw water over him and brought him awake, gasping. They amused themselves kicking or beating him, but after a while the slop they were drinking had them staggering, colliding with each other in uncontrolled meanderings. One or two men actually fell down and passed out right then and there. The off-key singing of obscene ditties gradually died and someone complained loudly in barely intelligible words, that 'the last of the lousy likker was finished – gone! Pissed agin the rocks . . .'

The words trailed off and the man folded up. As alert as he could make himself now, Cole Adams looked at the bodies of the outlaws scattered around the camp-fire, which was only glowing coals by now. There were seven of them, including Taylor himself and the guard from the entrance who had come in complaining that they were drinking all the whiskey while he was expected to stay awake and . . .

He had been in time to down enough to make him

as sleepy or as drunk as the others.

Seven men – seven he had to kill . . .

Cole held that thought, forced it back every time it started to drift away when pain or exhaustion threatened to overwhelm him. How he was going to do it, he had no idea. But it would happen! *It had to!*

Somehow, maybe with a miracle, maybe by his own efforts, but somehow he would escape and live long enough to kill them all.

But just a few minutes of trying to twist his wrists in the bonds and he knew it was all a dream, as Taylor had said.

There was no way he was going to get out of this. They could torture him, shoot him to pieces, cut his ears off, do whatever they liked with him – and he was powerless to stop it. *Powerless – too well-restrained – weak.*

His dying would be hard and made a hundred times worse by the knowledge that he would never be able to avenge Barbara and the horrors she had endured at the hands of Leith Taylor.

The thought brought a dry, frustrated sob from him and he threw back his head, ignoring the hurt, trying to work up some sort of despairing cry to fling into the night in one final savage protest.

Then he froze.

Something gnawed at the ropes binding his right hand to the sapling and in moments his arm dropped limply beside him, the first searing pain of returning circulation starting almost immediately. He bit down on his lower lip.

Even as the first involuntary moan escaped his

battered lips, his left hand was cut free and it, too, fell like a dead, leaden weight against his bruised body.

And the returning blood flow sent burning pain through his shoulders and neck, filled his ears with roaring.

But instead of gritting his teeth or trying to smother gasps of pain, he began to shake and he realized with a shock that he was – *laughing*!

Softly – very, very softly, as he thought:

Did someone say something about a miracle?

CHAPTER 8

THE CROWDED HILLS

If she hadn't heard the distant gunshot – and recognized that it came from the direction of one of the pastures that Jimmy Cross was checking – Tess Fowler wasn't sure just what she might have done.

She had seen the man who called himself Cole Adams taken away – as a prisoner, no less – by the three armed men who had accosted him on the trail below where she stood behind the boulders. She didn't recognize any of the men but there was some harsh laughter and a voice said clearly enough:

'*We ain't from any posse, Adams – but by the time we're finished with you, you'll wish we were!*'

There was no doubt that Adams was in for some ill-treatment: she witnessed some of the casual brutality before they roped him into his saddle. She didn't know what to do about it, but worked her way back to her horse and that was when she heard the distant echoes of the gunshot, coming from the north-west pastures.

Tess couldn't tackle three men alone, wasn't even sure if she should interfere in any way at all. Suppose she managed to get the drop on them – what would she do then? Make them turn Adams loose, an accused murderer and thief already on the run? *Why* was she even contemplating interfering? If Adams was guilty of the crimes Nate Kendrick had accused him of, he deserved everything he got. Those men could have had loved ones killed by Adams – as her father had been, according to Nate Kendrick – during one of his violent robberies and were out for revenge. In which case she could understand their actions.

But there was something in the manner of those three strangers, waiting for Adams on the trail. She knew it was dangerous to form opinions of anyone simply by the way they looked but – those three seemed to her as if *they* should have been behind bars. *Maybe they were bounty hunters. . .?*

By this time, she was almost to the bottom of the ridge and ready to turn on to the trail that Jimmy Cross would have followed earlier on his way to inspect the herds.

Then she saw him, riding towards her at a fast clip. She waved and waited for him. 'Din' 'spect to meet you so soon, Tess. On my way to tell you I had to put down one of the steers. That damn loose fence Curly never fixed! I'll fire the son of a – wire'd cut right into the neck, steer would've bled to death anyway.' Tess nodded in understanding: it certainly wasn't good news but she had other things on her mind right then. She told Cross about Cole Adams and how he had been roughly handled before being led away, tied to his saddle horn. 'But from what those strangers said they were going to beat him up at least. Perhaps even torture him, Jimmy.'

'Well, if he's escaped jail and is on the run, it's his hard luck, way I see it.' No sympathy there for Adams.

She looked at her foreman hard and he frowned. 'Jimmy, I have a feeling about this Adams. When I saw him in jail I – I don't know what it was, but something – call it woman's intuition, if you like – but *something* told me he was not the man who murdered Dad.'

Jimmy Cross seemed uneasy now. He didn't want to laugh out loud – *woman's intuition*, for God's sake! – but he covered with a cough behind his hand and said, 'Well, I guess I better send someone to fetch the sheriff and find out what's really happenin'.'

'Wait! Suppose Adams *is* innocent and has been released? We'll lose all that time and he could be killed by the time Nate Kendrick gets here.'

'Ye-ah,' Cross said slowly, sensing what was coming next. 'It's – possible, I guess.'

'Jimmy, you're the best tracker on Lazy F. I want you to follow those men and—'

'Aw, now look, Tess, this is somethin' we oughtn't to get involved in. Nate Kendrick's paid to do this sort of chore.'

'I'm already involved! I – stood by and watched those men rough-up Adams, tie him to his saddle.'

'Well, hell, there wasn't anythin' you could do.'

'But I feel there was something I should've done, Jimmy. It's a very strong feeling and . . .'

He lifted his hat, scratched at his damp black hair. 'You're the boss, Tess, but . . . it could be dangerous. Why don't you go find Kendrick and I'll see if I can pick up the tracks of these other fellers, get an idea of where they're headed?'

'We'll do it together, Jimmy.'

He opened his mouth to argue but knew that stubborn look she got on her face at times – inherited from old Stonewall Fowler: no one ever got anyplace trying to argue with him and Jimmy knew from experience the same applied to his daughter.

So they rode warily, back over the ridge and down to where she had seen Adams sitting his black with hands raised.

Cross dismounted, studying the mess of churned-up ground and looked up at her, mouth grim. 'They were mighty rough with him, all right. Some blood here and there, drag marks, shirt-buttons, torn-off collar, and the rowel snapped off a spur. There was some sort of fracas here.'

'Can you make out where they were going?'

He pointed to the mountain rearing above, the base already in shadow.

They rode slowly, both with rifles out, but darkness caught up with them and they had to make camp for the night. They sheltered in a shallow cave and were on the trail again right after sunrise, Jimmy crouching low to utilize the early light that outlined the tracks more clearly.

They found the night-camp site that had been used by the outlaws and Adams but there was nothing useful left behind that could help them.

The ground was drying fast now and tracks were not so easy to pick up. It was a long, thirsty, hungry day and they realized they were in a section of the hills that neither of them knew very well. Cross could pick out landmarks he had heard of or seen marked on sparsely detailed survey maps, but had never actually been within sight of them until now. And it reached a point in the afternoon when they just had to rest their mounts, still not certain of their whereabouts.

At least they found a spring, but Cross advised against a camp-fire.

So they ate leather-tough jerky and washed it down with spring water. They were smoothing out their sleeping places when Cross suddenly held up a hand, paused in unbuckling a strap securing his bedroll. Tess heard it then, very faint, but so alien in these hills that it demanded attention.

It was someone singing – more than one. They sounded drunk and, while she couldn't make out the words, she thought she recognized the tune of a well-known cowboy ditty whose words were not usually meant for female ears.

'They got a camp somewheres close. I'd say other side of the ridge. That's what's mufflin' the singin'.'

After a short discussion – not quite an argument – he agreed she should ride to the top of the ridge with him.

'If we see a camp-fire, you stay with the hosses while I scout around.'

Tess agreed, and when they reached the crest the outlaws' camp was easy to see, only fifty yards down-slope on a wide grassy bench, studded here and there with rock clumps.

They could easily see Adams roped to his yoke – and, at irregular intervals being subjected to the violent whims of the seven men drinking from a stone jug, sitting around the dying camp-fire. Occasionally one staggered over and kicked or beat Adams about the head.

'They'll kill him!' Tess whispered but Jimmy's hand grabbed her arm swiftly and hard.

'No. They could've done it long ago if that's all they wanted. They're havin' fun with him first . . .'

'Fun!'

'Keep your voice down, dammit!' he hissed not even bothering to apologize for speaking to her in that manner. 'Look, a couple've passed out already. They'll be all snorin' in a little while. I'll go down and see if I can find where they've got their horses and maybe I'll be able to do somethin' about Adams.'

She detected something in his voice but couldn't see well enough in the dark to read his expression.

'You don't like what's happening down there, do you. Jim?'

'No, even my Cherokee blood don't like seein' a helpless man beat up and tortured that way. Now you stay put, but be ready to ride. If they catch me, get the hell out and find Kendrick. If I'm lucky, I'll be back and I'll likely be comin' fast, so keep the broncs ready to go . . .'

'I'll be ready, Jimmy.'

He hoped like hell she would be: he didn't fancy tangling with those sadistic bastards down there.

*

Twenty minutes later the camp-fire had burned down to glowing ashes and Leith Taylor and his crew were sprawled all over the grass, snoring in drunken sleep.

Within minutes, the bloody Adams was startled to feel his wrist bonds being cut away and, right after, his ankle ropes.

'Who?' he rasped as the dark shadow of his rescuer moved to grab him under the armpits, knowing his limbs would be numbed after having been bound up for so long.

'*Shut up!*' Cross hissed and began the slow, awkward and back-breaking job of getting Adams away from the camp without disturbing the outlaws.

Cross wasn't a particularly big man but he was wiry and strong. Even so, he was staggering, breathing like a locomotive labouring up a mountain gradient by the time he reached Tess Fowler. She helped him ease the semi-conscious Adams to the ground, seeing streaks of blood glinting dully on his battered face.

'Did you get him a horse?'

Because of the darkness, she was unable to see the burning look of naked hostility Cross threw her way. *Bossy damn women!* But he managed to keep his tone more or less normal – with plenty of gasping as he fought for breath.

'They're hobbled on the grass below the camp. I – I'll go see if I can get one.'

'He was riding a black . . .'

Christ! I don't care if he was riding Pegasus, he'll take whatever I can get. That was what the nearly exhausted Cross thought; aloud, he said: 'I'll see what I can do.'

He faded into the darkness and she heard him

slithering and sliding down the slope, hoped the sounds wouldn't wake the sleeping outlaws. But the rotgut had done its work well and no one stirred.

She was on edge and impatient by the time he returned, leading a chestnut with a saddle.

'Didn't you see his black?'

'No, dammit! I just caught the first hoss within reach and grabbed the nearest saddle. Lucky, too. There's a rifle in the scabbard. Now let's get the hell out of here.'

'Are the horses still hobbled or. . . ?'

'Tess! We don't have time for discussion, but, no, I cut their hobbles and they'll be miles away come morning. I also cut the cinch straps on the saddles – now, for God's sake, *let's get out of here*!'

The posse's venture into the Saddlebacks was not very successful until the men under Renny Kendrick stumbled across the tracks of Adams's black gelding. Renny's first instinct was to fire a shot as a signal to bring his father's part of the posse to him. But a couple of the townsmen pointed out that, because the trail led to the point where Adams had been accosted by the three outlaws, they were likely some of his gang-members waiting for him, and could be still close enough to hear any gunshots. Renny seemed irritated and for a moment made to draw his pistol and signal anyway. But the posse showed so much hostility that at last he sullenly agreed and sent a man to fetch his father.

'Looks to me like he met someone he knew here and they took off into the hills, Pa. Lots of tracks,'

Renny said when Nate showed. Renny had been examining the cut in his head again in his mirror and was in the act of patting the waves back in place when Nate arrived and snarled,

'Put that goddamn mirror away! Judas, boy, ain't you got any sense? Who the hell cares if your hair's mussed out here? The sun could reflect off that thing and warn the outlaws! You can bet they've got a look-out someplace!'

Renny flushed and mumbled, 'Sorry, Pa!'

A retired Army scout, Frenchy Lucas, had been hired as tracker by Nate. He straightened now to his full five feet six inches, pulled at his long nose, and said, 'Sign here could've been made by a scuffle. Someone fell or was dragged off a hoss. Rest is all churned up and changes shape as the mud slid away down slope before the rain stopped.'

'You sayin' whoever he met might not've been friendly?' Sheriff Kendrick demanded and at Frenchy's nod, Nate scowled. 'No one but us knows about his escape. Might've just been the hosses actin' up, made that mess of tracks. Look: it's right on the edge of a drop and you can see where the edges've broke away.'

Frenchy shrugged. Twenty years in the army had taught him it was useless to argue with the man in charge. Anyway, he was being paid by the day: if they didn't want to listen to him it made no nevermind to him. The longer it took, the more he earned.

'We follow these tracks and see if the black's are among 'em.' That was Nate's decision.

It was easy enough to find the tracks of Adams's horse amongst the others, but then the ground hardened and Frenchy really had to start earning his pay. The sign was there to read if you knew what to look for in this type of country. Frenchy had been rebuffed once so he didn't put forth any theories, merely reported what he found.

'Tracks lead up there – over the ridge.'

'All four are still together in a group,' Nate said with something of a smirk, sure Adams had rejoined his gang.

'Don't mean they're friendly,' muttered Frenchy.

They wound their way up and over the ridge and Frenchy, scouting on ahead, found the outlaws' camp on the grassy bench and the area where the mounts had been hobbled below. He brought back with him some short, wide lengths of leather.

'Cinch straps. Someone cut 'em and any fool knows that ain't no friendly gesture.'

'What're you sayin'?' demanded Nate.

'Someone run off the mounts – and there must've been eight or ten, I reckon, likely a couple bein' packhosses.'

'Then, if this was where Adams's gang was camped, they must be afoot chasin' their hosses!' Renny said brightly but his smugness faded at the pitying look on Frenchy's face.

'Any half-wit can join a cut cinch with a doubled length of rope! Might give the bronc a sore belly, but a man can ride just as comfortable.'

By that time someone had found the blood-spattered yoke and the cut ropes. Nate scratched his head.

'They had someone prisoner and give him a bad time.'

89

Frenchy, coming back from a dry wash where the stampeded mounts had run, nodded. 'You'll be happy to know, Adams's black is with the hosses that run off.'

That brightened the sheriff no end. 'I knew it! This must be the gang's hideout! They busted him out and he met 'em, and now they've cleared out 'cause they know I'll have posses all through these hills.'

'There's that bloody saplin' – and someone did turn the mounts loose,' Frenchy pointed out.

'Yeah. That's puzzlin', but by hell, long as Adams's black's with the rest of the hosses it means he's there, too, so we're gonna follow.'

'Mightn't hurt to split up, Nate. Just in case.'

Kendrick scowled at the old tracker. 'Tell you what, Frenchy, you go scout around wherever you want. Me, I'm takin' the posse wherever them tracks lead – and I'll guarantee we'll find Adams and the other sons of bitches who've been doin' all the robberies and murders!'

It sounded OK to the possemen: they knew *they* could share in the big rewards even if the lawmen didn't qualify.

Frenchy was going to point out that it didn't necessarily have to be Adams riding the black gelding but, what the hell? He decided he might as well ride with the posse.

If know-all Nate got them lost in the hills, Frenchy would be the one who would have to find a way out.

And he'd damn well take his time doing it, too.

CHAPTER 9

MAN HUNTERS

A hangover from hastily brewed, unfiltered moonshine was bad enough, Leith Taylor thought as his horse put a forefoot into yet another hole on the rough trail. The jarring surged right through his suffering body and seemed to lift the top of his skull several inches away from his throbbing brain.

His eyeballs felt loose in their sockets and he squeezed them tight shut even as he snarled bitter curses at his mount, jerking the reins, sawing at the animal's mouth. Naturally, it resented such treatment, whinnied in protest, stomped its feet, swayed violently, threw back its head, which almost collided with Taylor's misshapen face.

'Judas priest, Leith!' called Crewe, who was riding just behind and suddenly had his own hands full of stomping, jerking horse. 'The hell're you doin'!'

'If we had any spare mounts, I'd cut this son of a bitch's throat!' Taylor broke off, frowning, putting a hand up to his pounding temples. 'Who the hell made that moonshine this time?'

'Taft. He told you it wasn't ready but because we had Adams all roped up, you wanted a celebration an'—'

'All right, all right! Jesus – some celebration.'

Crewe put his mount up alongside Taylor's, which had quietened down now.

'We lost a lot of time gettin' our mounts back, Leith. It'll be dark soon and we still ain't sure we're still headed in the right direction.'

'You got a better direction? Then spit it out! I dunno any other way to go, for Chrissakes! The trail led in this general direction before we lost it . . .'

'Because whoever rescued him was smart enough and good enough to cover it up,' Crewe opined and earned another vitriolic curse from Taylor. 'Had to be that way, Leith – just suddenly stopped on the crest of the ridge. Led nowhere.'

'Yeah, yeah, I know. So we had two choices, didn't we? Go down on the north side, or down on the south. We split and Trigger comes back without findin' one lousy sign! But we found what could be sign, a broken ridge of dirt with what looked like the curve of a horseshoe on the edge.'

'Which crumbled as soon as we touched it. I still reckon it was a rounded stone that made that curve, not a horseshoe at all.'

Crewe reared back suddenly as Taylor's sixgun appeared and the man's drink-ravaged face was about as ugly as he'd ever seen it – or wanted to.

'Crewe – *shut the hell up*! I am fed up with arguin''

92

with you. We – found – sign – and we're gonna follow the general direction. No more discussion! None!'

That was all right with Crewe and he let out the breath he had been holding when Taylor lowered the gun hammer and dropped the Colt back in its holster.

The rest of the gang were strung out along the narrow trail they were riding and just as they started off again, the last man in line, the squat Punkin, half-standing in his stirrups, yelled,

'Leith! A posse! A goddamned posse comin' over the crest!'

His words got the attention of every man there and there were curses and goosebumps and cramping bellies when they saw how many riders were putting their mounts down the steep slope above and to their left.

'Must've deputized half the goddamn town!' Taft exclaimed.

Before they could act, four or five guns crackled in the fading light and one of the outlaws was flung from his horse, his body hitting the trail on the steep side, rolling down out of sight, dead before he'd stopped sliding.

By then Taylor and Crewe and the others were spurring recklessly along the narrow trail, reaching for their guns, bullets buzzing and whipping air around them.

'Scatter!' yelled Taylor but there was nowhere to scatter to on this trail: no one seemed eager to set their mounts with the makeshift cinches down such a steep slope.

They all wanted to follow the vague trail they had been using. One rider, impatient, slammed his horse – Cole Adams's black as it happened – up alongside the man in front. There was only room for one rider at a time here and the man riding the black made sure he was uppermost on the grade. The one being shouldered aside looked up with startled eyes and brought his sixgun around, shooting.

He was too panicky and triggered too soon. The bullet dusted the wide brim of the man on the black – a flabby-gutted rider called Soupbone – and then the muscular black, surefooted, thrust into position, rammed into the other horse. It shrilled and jerked and the outlaw in the saddle screamed as both man and mount went off the edge.

The horse's legs folded and one snapped like a gunshot. The outlaw sailed over the head and crashed into a deadfall on the slope. The posse came thundering down, spread out on the higher slopes now, guns hammering.

Taylor, looking out for Leith Taylor as usual, hit a bend and was first to see a possible escape route. There was a washaway that dropped into a small cutting, ten or twelve feet of fairly steep slope, loose earth studded with rocks.

The other way, the narrow trail continued without any sign of widening, straight as an arrow shaft: the posse could pick them off at their leisure along that stretch.

It took Leith about two seconds to decide that here was a chance that had either to be taken right now or missed for ever.

94

His horse squealed in protest as he cuffed it with his gloved hand, causing it to jerk left at just the right moment. It would never have made the leap voluntarily but, instinctively moving to get away from the blow near its eye, it moved in the direction Taylor wanted. The earth was softer than he'd expected. The mount's forefeet dug in – and in – and in – and for a moment the outlaw thought he was going to be thrown over the mount's head. But the horse dropped its haunches and somehow achieved a more or less even keel and began to slide down into the cutting, snorting, wild-eyed.

Outlaw gunfire brought down two posse men and a third's horse reared and backed off, hit in the rump. Bullets churned the slope around the escaping Taylor. He didn't bother trying to return fire: he stretched out along his mount's back. All he wanted to do was get the hell out of there, preferably with a whole hide.

It surprised him to see out of the corner of his eye that Crewe was coming after him, fighting his horse, but still in the saddle. Another outlaw, Punkin, tried but was thrown heavily, skidding on his back for several yards before struggling to his feet – just in time to be cut down by a shot from Nate Kendrick's Winchester.

One other outlaw hit the slope and managed to control his horse. The others were shot out of leather by the manhunters, who seemed to take up most of the high ground above now.

'Don't let 'em get away!' bawled Nate Kendrick, working his rifle lever only to find that the magazine was empty.

Most of the other posse members on this part of the slope were running out, too. Only three single shots were fired and then the men had to try to reload whilst riding. Two dismounted to tend the wounded posse men, hearing Nate swear. The outlaws who had reached the cutting by now were almost out of range and would be hidden by a jutting rockface.

Kendrick fumed and roared at the men whose guns still held cartridges to get after the outlaws. One man tried, spurring his mount, leaping it out on to the loose slope. It snapped both forelegs and the rider broke his shoulder. The others reined up and looked at the sheriff, still thumbing fresh loads into his rifle. He nodded resignedly.

'All right. It's dangerous, I know, but we still go after 'em. These are the sonuvers who busted Adams outta jail – and I want the whole blamed lot of 'em before I give up! Now, get your broncs down there somehow – and don't waste any more time!'

Renny was close by and Frenchy was studying the slope, looking for the safest place to start the descent, when Nate said to his son,

'You see that son of a bitch on the black? He weren't wearin' no checked shirt, but I reckon it was Adams, all right.'

'We-ell, I dunno, Pa. I didn't get a clear look.'

' 'Course it weren't Adams!' Frenchy cut in curtly. 'Hell almighty, that feller had a gut on him like a beer keg! Adams is straight up and down like a ramrod.'

Nate glared. 'I know what I saw! In any case –

96

Adams has to be with them!'

'No he don't. Whyn't you check the ones we nailed? One of 'em might still be alive. Can tell you for sure.'

The sheriff growled at Renny. 'You shoulda thought of that! Get off your damn hoss and go check them fellers lyin' on the slope. If one's alive – well, he'll talk before the sun goes down behind these hills! You got my word on that.'

Renny sighed and dismounted. Nate said to Frenchy: 'Your idea. Go lend him a hand.'

'Dammit, you think I can't find a couple wounded outlaws an' bring 'em back? Stay with your trackin', Frenchy – for all the damn use it is.' Renny stomped off, fuming.

Frenchy pursed his lips, swivelled his gaze to Nate, who was looking at his son, puzzled.

'Reckon the boy needs to be a mite more independent, Nate.'

Kendrick started to bristle. 'When I want your advice—' He snapped his mouth closed, nodded jerkily. 'Mebbe you're right. He's been actin' kinda queer for a while now, like he's got a mad-on at the whole damned world. Bitchin' I don't pay him enough, workin' hours are too long – then says I don't give him enough real jobs, whatever the hell he thinks they are.' He shook his head. 'A real pain in the ass. Even threatened to turn in his badge, but I won't stand for that! I'm his father and he'll do what I tell him or—'

'Give him a little more rein, Nate.'

This time the sheriff glared. 'Like Renny said, get

on with your trackin', Frenchy! You leave raisin' my son to me.'

Frenchy nodded and squatted down again, saying half-aloud, 'It sure better be left to someone who knows how to handle him. That boy's gettin' ready to *bust.*'

A few minutes later they heard gunshots and, as all the posse looked down the slope, Renny appeared with a smoking pistol.

'Three of 'em, Pa. First one's dead as a fish in a desert. One of the others tried to reach his sixgun, so I finished him off. Then made sure of the last one while I was at it.'

'Well, ain't that a real smart thing to do!' Nate shouted angrily. 'Christ, boy, they might've told us *somethin'!*'

'Mighta shot me, too!' Renny replied hotly. 'What'll I do with the bodies?'

'Leave 'em to the wolves. We've wasted enough time.'

Frenchy walked up to the sheriff, protest on his ugly old face even before he spoke. 'Now that ain't right, Nate. The slope's not all that hard. They can be at least covered with some dirt.'

'You just got the job – if it means that much to you.' Nate Kendrick snapped, turning away.

'Well, I'd like to think someone'd bury me if I die in the wilderness. I ain't got no notion to be turned into coyote crap.'

A couple of posse men murmured agreement but Frenchy started down alone, passing Renny slogging his way back up.

'Two of 'em's strangers, but feller I had to kill was Punkin Peters.'

Frenchy grunted. '*Had* to kill him, did you?'

'Hell, he was reachin' for his Colt! Was him or me! Renny snapped and kept on climbing back up the slope.

Frenchy found the first man who had a broken neck as well as three bullets in his body, any one of which could have been fatal: there was no way he could have survived. The second man had a mortal wound, too, but Renny had put a bullet through his heart to make sure. Punkin Peters, the one Renny claimed had gone for his Colt, was further along and down at the bottom of the slope. He had been shot high in the chest and there was a still-oozing wound in his head from Renny's bullet.

Looked to Frenchy like it was a waste of powder and lead. Punkin might've been able to mutter something, but Frenchy doubted it: that wound high in the chest would've torn up his vocal chords for one thing and he'd sure bled a hell of a lot. Wouldn't have lasted another ten minutes, maybe only five.

Anyway, Renny had made absolutely sure with that head shot: he hadn't lasted even one extra minute.

The old scout picked up a dead branch and began digging at the loose earth, scraping it down over the bodies with his cupped hands and arms, stomping it firmly with his feet. As he did so, he noticed Punkin's sixgun holster – it was empty.

There was no sign of the gun anywhere on the lower slopes or near where Punkin's body had been.

But a ray of the fast-westering sun glinted off blued

steel way up near the trail above – just about where a thrown rider's Colt would have jarred loose from its holster.

Frenchy paused in his grave-digging, scratched his head under his battered campaign hat.

'Never knew ol' Punkin had such long arms,' he murmured, before continuing with his grim chore.

CHAPTER 10

"WE'LL FIND HIM!"

'What've you done to your hair? It's darker than it was.'

Tess Fowler, opening the door to leave the room, was startled, not just by the question, but the fact that the voice sounded so strong. She turned quickly, closed the door, looked back at the man in the narrow bed, now struggling to sit up.

She set down the wooden tray with the uneaten food on it and hurried to the bedside, gently but firmly forcing Cole Adams down against the pillows.

'Just lie still! The doctor has your ribs strapped up because he's afraid at least one may be splintered and if you move around too much it could damage your lungs – or other organs.'

Cole looked up at her, his left eye only partly open, the lid and the flesh underneath coloured purple and a sickly yellow at the edges. His nose was broken but had been set by someone who knew what they were doing – Cole used to earn drinking money as a tent-fighter in medicine shows and bare-fist bouts with all comers. His nose had been hammered into many weird shapes during that time, nearly always set indifferently. His mouth was lopsided but the swelling was going down. His upper body felt like a horse had stomped on it and even his arms ached and throbbed as if they had been clamped in a vice, especially his red, raw wrists.

He glanced around the sparsely furnished room with the vertical bare-board walls, yellowed with age and considerable tobacco smoke, he guessed. He started to ask where he was but saw the girl's face clearly for the first time, and said sharply, 'You're not Barbara!'

Tess Fowler placed a cool soft hand across his scarred brow and smiled down at him. 'No, I'm Tess. I own the Lazy F ranch – we met in Gallant – in the—'

'In the jail!' he interrupted, started to try to struggle to a sitting position again but she held him expertly down on the mattress.

'Now stop that! Or I'll have to strap you down again.'

He blinked. 'Again?'

'Yes. You've been struggling, talking a lot of nonsense and sweating for a couple of days and we had to keep you still, so you had to be strapped down – on the doctor's orders, I might add.'

He nodded slowly. 'Yeah. Coming back to me now. Sort of. Someone tossed me a gun through the bars. Know now it was a feller named Crewe – runs with an outlaw bunch under Leith Taylor.'

'I – don't know who you're talking about.'

'No, well you wouldn't. Taylor's the one in the flour-sack hood who's been dropping my name at all the robberies and killings he's done.'

She frowned slightly. 'I – we only saw half a dozen or so men sprawled out on that grassy bench, obviously sleeping off, drunk. Are they the ones you mean?'

'That's them. I tangled with Taylor about five years ago.' His voice changed and she saw the memories working on his face. 'I was clearing land on our quarter-section, away from the cabin. Barbara was home alone when Taylor came by, on the run as it turned out . . .' He went quiet and she waited him out, seeing him reliving the horror in his mind. 'She was just over seven months pregnant and the ba— – he did all kinds of things to her. I almost killed him with my bare hands when I got back to the cabin. Only the posse arriving saved Taylor. Kinda strange when you think about it: the law saving an outlaw. And that did no one any favours.'

Her hand squeezed his shoulder gently and his mouth moved in the faintest of smiles of appreciation. 'I messed up his face. Heard he'd been killed in the territorial prison – but he escaped and he's after me.'

'He – he deliberately mentioned your name while he was committing all these crimes? To – get back at you for disfiguring him?'

'That was the idea – the more he mentioned my name, the more notorious I became, which meant a bigger bounty.'

She waited, not quite understanding.

'He didn't know where I was but because of the crimes he framed me for, I was worth almost twelve thousand dollars, dead or alive. He had men watching out for me. One happened to be in the barbershop in Gallant. I dunno if he recognized me, but I'd already signed the assayer's book and he went and told Kendrick. Renny threw me in jail, which made it easy for Taylor because he knew just where to find me. Then they dropped that gun through the bars, knowing I'd bust out, and picked me up in those hills because there was nowhere else for me to run. Taylor decided to have a little fun with me before he turned me in – dead – and collected what he calls *his* money.'

She put one small hand to her mouth, astounded.

'But that – that's . . .' she was lost for the word she wanted, but her shoulders shuddered as if she had felt a sudden chill. 'My God, that's the mind of a madman!'

'Mebbe. But it could've worked. We're about the same size. No one knew my face, only my name. There would be plenty of folk ready to swear I was the one robbed them – or killed some member of their family.'

Their gazes locked as he said this and she nodded gently. 'Like my father being shot down at my side. I was almost ready to tell Nate Kendrick I thought you were the one who did it but something stopped me. I have no idea what it was – but – well, I'm glad I didn't accuse you.' Her voice was suddenly sharp. 'At least, I hope I did the right thing.'

'You did. I've told you the truth. I've been prop-

104

secting up in the hills for almost a year. Knew nothing about being a wanted man or any of those robberies.'

'Were you alone?'

'Had an old sourdough prospector with me for a spell, but he died.'

Disappointment straightened her face. 'Then there's no one who could swear you were nowhere near any of the places where Taylor committed his crimes?'

He shrugged and it hurt his side a little. She was immediately concerned. 'It's OK. Just wasn't ready for it. But I could sure use a cup of coffee and – maybe a couple or three fried eggs?'

Her smile brightened the room more than the sunshine.

'I've been waiting for you to say something like that!' She indicated the tray with the cold food and coffee on it. 'You haven't been conscious enough to take any food.'

'I'm – mighty obliged for all you've done, ma'am. Who was it got me away from Taylor?'

'My ramrod – Jimmy Cross.'

'Sure like to shake his hand.'

'That'll come soon enough,' she told him, still smiling as she went out of the room.

Later that evening, after another big meal, Cole Adams told Jimmy Cross about Leith Taylor and what he had done to Barbara all those years ago.

'I knew there was owlhoots hangin' about our hills,' Cross said in that slow, thoughtful way he spoke. 'Seen tracks often enough but I usually ride alone and – well, didn't fancy my chances against a bunch of men who lived by their guns.'

'Don't blame you, specially with Taylor's crew.'

'Well, I doubt they'll be back to that hideout – there's a big posse scourin' the country for 'em and Nate Kendrick is about the stubbornest coot I know – though Tess's pa weren't called 'Stonewall' for nothin', and she takes after him that way.'

They grinned and Cole suddenly reached for Cross's cigarette and took a drag on it. The smoke tasted good going down but once in his lungs a fit of coughing almost tore him apart. The ramrod, in a state of concern that was closely alllied to straight-out panic, shouted for Tess. She came bustling in, throwing Cross an angry look.

'I told you he wasn't to smoke yet!'

'It was just one drag. . . !'

Adams got control of his coughing, waved the girl away. 'Don't blame – Jimmy. I just took it outta his hand.'

She looked exasperated and shook her head. 'Men!'

That single word said a lot about her opinion of them.

Wanting to change the subject, Cole asked, 'Your men know I'm here? Guess they must do.'

'We came in very late at night, in fact, well after midnight. I only have three or four men – it varies with the work – and they were all asleep in the bunkhouse. Jimmy and I got you up here into my father's old room without anyone being the wiser.'

'But – the sawbones visiting. . . ?'

'My riders don't come up to the house. I told them an old friend coming to see me had taken a bad fall from his horse and I was caring for him. Besides, Doc Hartwell is an old family friend, used to visit often with my father. Seeing him come to Lazy F is nothing for the crew to get curious about. They've seen him visit many times before.'

Adams looked sceptical.

'Don't worry. Not one of them is interested enough to ask any more questions – and we're on the upper floor of the house here so no one'll be peeking in the window.'

'Which means when you get mobile again,' said Cross, 'you stay away from it.' He nodded to the window, which now had a blind drawn down.

Adams frowned even as he nodded. 'What about the posses? If the law finds me here you're gonna be in one helluva fix, Tess.'

'If they come here – and I said if – I'll give them supplies, even remounts, and a meal – but it will all take place in the barn or the bunkhouse.'

Adams looked from one to the other. 'It's damn risky for you both. I'll get out of your hair quick as I can.'

She leaned down. and lightly slapped his face, more a pat than a slap. 'You'll stay put until I say you're fit to leave. Doc Hartwell has given me strict instructions what I'm to do – and I'll only call him in an emergency. All you have to do is what you're told and if you do that, you'll be fit again all the sooner.'

He still didn't like it.

He liked it even less when early, two mornings

later, the door opened part way and Tess poked her head in, speaking in a loud whisper.

'Make sure you stay away from the window and don't make a sound.'

He tensed. 'What's happened?'

'The sheriff is downstairs, asking about that chestnut Jimmy took from the outlaws so we could bring you here.'

'Well, wha. . . ?'

But she was gone, closing the door softly. He heard her footsteps hurrying towards the stairs at the end of the short hallway.

His heart was hammering against his ribs – and there wasn't a gun in sight. If the law walked in here now, he was as good as dead.

'Just wandered in, you say?'

Sheriff Nate Kendrick was standing in the shadow of the big barn, smoking and holding a cup of coffee brought to him by the cook. The other posse members had dismounted, were scattered around the yard and corrals, also with coffee, glad to have something decent to drink instead of the wild brews they had swallowed on the trail. Tess's crew were already out on the range, but Jimmy Cross had one boot up on the end of a horse trough, elbow resting across his bent leg, cigarette burning between his fingers. Tess stood in the shade cast by the early sun, watching Nate Kendrick's trail-worn, creased and dirt-caked face.

'You look like you've had a rough trail, Nate,' she said. 'Why don't you clean up at the washbench? The cook'll be finished making breakfast by then and—'

'Like to take you up on that, Tess, but a mite later. I'm interested in this chestnut.'

Frenchy Lucas strolled across and leaned against the wall a few feet away, sipping a mug of coffee. Cross knew the old scout's ear was hanging out a mile.

'Yes – we found it outside the corrals one morning.' She turned to the foreman. 'Day before yesterday, Jimmy?'

'That's right. He musta sensed our horses and came in. Sure was hungry but he looks way better now since we curry-combed him.'

'No sign of a rider?'

Cross shook his head. 'Not even a saddle.'

Frenchy turned his head quickly but made no comment.

The ramrod had taken the saddle off the horse after he and Tess had carried Adams up to bed. He had not cut the cinchstrap on that one at the outlaw camp, but he buried it beneath a pile of old ranch junk just in case someone recognized it.

Nate scratched at his stubble and Renny strolled across, juggling a hot golden-brown biscuit from one hand to another. 'Hey, Pa! These are the best biscuits I've ever tasted. Any chance of takin' a batch with us, Tess?'

'You'll have to ask Cookie, but if he has enough I'm sure he'll give you some.'

Renny grinned around a mouthful and went towards the cook shack. Nate glared after him.

'Like a damn big kid! Thinkin' of his belly at a

time like this.' He sighed. 'Well, Tess, reckon we'll have us some breakfast and a wash and move along. If you got any sowbelly an' flour to spare, and maybe some coffee beans. . . ?'

'I've just stocked up, Nate, so you're lucky. You and the men make yourselves at home. I'll fix you a grubsack.'

Cross straightened and said, 'I'll get a couple more washbasins so you won't take so long.'

'Wantin' rid of us, Jimmy?' Kendrick asked and although there was a tired grin on his face, there was just enough edge to the words to make Tess feel tense.

'You're the one seems to be in a hurry,' Jimmy Cross answered. 'You checkin' all the ranches?'

Nate's gaze was steady. 'Not yet. You're the first.'

'And to what do we owe that . . . honour, Nate?' Tess asked, hoping the question sounded like mere light curiosity.

'You can blame Old Hawkeye there.' He gestured to Frenchy. 'He noticed in the outlaw camp the prints of eight horses – but the gang we jumped only had seven. So he scouted around and found a few tracks, one that came from the camp – and eventually led us here, to the chestnut.'

'You haven't lost your touch, Frenchy,' Tess complimented him and the old scout looked briefly pleased.

'Wearin' the brand Diamond K/L.'

Tess frowned. 'I don't think I know it.'

'Not surprisin',' Nate said. 'It was stolen a year ago from outside the cathouse in Wellington – long ways from here. Likely most of the other broncs them outlaws were ridin' are stolen stock, too, eh, Frenchy?'

The old scout said nothing, just stayed put, still sipping his coffee. Tess noticed he was taking a long time to drink it and this only added to her tension.

'Not having much success in finding your escapee, Nate?' she asked, just to fill in the silence that had developed and made her feel uneasy.

'We'll find him! But ain't just him now. He's with his gang. Seems they been hidin' out in the Saddlebacks an' that's where he was makin' for after he broke out. Guess they were celebratin' his return or somethin'. They seemed well hung-over when we jumped 'em.'

'We wouldn't't've gotten near 'em otherwise,' Frenchy allowed but no one took any notice. 'Not Taylor's bunch.'

'Then you're sure this Adams is with them?'

Frenchy stirred and cleared his throat as Kendrick said curtly, 'Hell, yeah! I seen him ridin' that black hoss of his when they gave us the slip.' He shook his head. 'Man, they was scared! The way they dived off that trail and down that slope!' He blew out his cheeks, glanced at Frenchy. 'Made the hackles stand up on the back of your neck, didn't it, Frenchy?'

'They were desperate, all right. But I still ain't sure it was Adams on that black, Nate.'

'Damnit, don't start that again!' Nate tossed his coffee dregs on the ground with an angry movement. 'C'mon – let's eat and wash up and get ridin'.'

'Your men must be tired,' Tess said. 'Wanting to

get back to their families.'

Nate glared. 'They'll stay till I tell 'em they can go home! This Adams made me look a fool and no man does that! When we ride back to Gallant, I'll have him with us – in manacles. Or roped over a hoss so's his body won't fall off!'

CHAPTER 11

RECOVERY

'You were told to stay away from that window!'

Tess was angry with Adams as he sat on the edge of the bed, obviously distressed from getting up.

'Just – took a – peek,' he told her breathlessly. 'Didn't know they had Lu-cah working for 'em.' He saw her frown. 'The old army scout.'

'Oh, Frenchy Lucas.'

He smiled thinly. 'Claims his folks were from France and his name's pronounced 'Lu-cah'. But makes no difference how you say it, if he's with that posse, he'll find me somehow and I'll have more trouble than you can shake a stick at.'

'I thought you already had that much trouble.' She was regretting her anger with him and helped him back under the covers. She knew he was trying not to show discomfort but heard the smothered grunts of pain as she arranged the pillows.

'He's a top tracker. Don't surprise me to know he

picked up those extra hoofprints made by the chestnut.' He looked at her a little more sharply. 'You might think you've settled with him, but I know him from way back. Did a stretch in the cavalry one time – and once he gets his teeth into something he don't let go.'

'Nate Kendrick seemed satisfied.'

'He's a different kettle of fish. Nate might think he's running that posse but it'll come down to Frenchy in the end. He can't get Nate to agree to something, he'll just ride on out – and do it his way. He won't quit. He'll just keep on till he's satisfied, one way or t'other.'

She frowned. 'You sound – very serious.'

'Told you, I know Frenchy Lu-cah, or Lucas, if you want.'

'He's retired now, too old for the army. Nate's hired him by the day.'

Cole's smile widened. 'Then he'll stretch it out a mite so he'll get more pay, 'cause you can bet any pension from the army won't give him much of a life.'

'Well, the posse's gone now and I've given them some supplies, so they'll be scouting through the hills again for at least another few days.'

'Then I'll have to get fit enough to ride out in that time.'

Tess showed her alarm at his words. 'Don't be so foolish, Cole Adams! Those ribs can cause you serious trouble and—'

'Ribs are OK.' She went to interrupt but he held up a hand. 'They're my ribs and I've had 'em splin-

114

tered before. I know the feeling. These aren't damaged. Likely the sawbones was just being cautious. Guess I ought to thank him for that. No, Tess! I know what I'm talking about. I'll be out of here in a few days and you'll have nothing more to worry about. Just stick to your story about that chestnut and Kendrick can't do a thing to you.'

She shook her head rather sadly from side to side. 'And Jimmy Cross has the cheek to say that I've inherited my father's well-known stubbornness! Obviously he hasn't had much to do with you, Cole Adams!'

'Not stubborn – just speaking from experience, Tess, Right now, I wouldn't care to try to hold a couple of pounds of iron, like a Colt revolver, let alone fire it. But I've got to get fit enough to do that, and use a rifle again.'

'Doc Hartwell says you've damaged the right shoulder, too.'

'I know! Hell, do I know! But I'll pad the rifle butt, maybe even low-load the shells.' At her puzzled look, he said, 'Take out a few grains of powder so there's not such a kick when it fires. I've done all this kind of thing before, Tess. Gospel.'

He saw the wariness in her face now and smiled again. 'No, I'm not an outlaw, never have been one, but after Barbara died I – I went kind of wild for quite a time. Put away a lot of booze, got into a lot of fights – would wake up in a ditch somewhere all beat up, or have a winning hand at poker and be too drunk to read the signs that someone was gonna roll me for the money. I've been three parts dead but it

115

didn't stop me crawling into some bar and drinking the dregs in the bottles waiting to be trashed.'

'It – must've been horrible!' She showed much more compassion than distaste, adding quietly, 'And you must have loved Barbara very much.'

He merely nodded and she knew enough not to pursue the subject.

'Long time ago. Just about long enough for me to forget most of the bad stuff – then Leith Taylor shows up again! Brings it all back.'

She reached out and gently adjusted a pillow to a more comfortable position.

'You're welcome to stay as long as you need to, Cole. You be the one to decide when you leave. I guess you'll know when that time comes.'

He was surprised at her words – and grateful, too. More than he could tell her right now.

Nate Kendrick walked over to one of the camp-fires where the weary posse men sat, eating, huddling close to the flames for it was cold in these hills after the sun went down.

Renny looked up, swallowing the last mouthful of the last biscuit the Lazy F cook had given him: he had hogged the lot and some of the men resented it, Nate included.

'Where the hell's Frenchy?' he demanded.

'Rode out a little while back,' Renny said helpfully.

'Where?'

The snarled word should have warned him his father was in one of his edgy moods, but with a full stomach and still the taste of those great biscuits in his mouth, he merely shrugged. He howled when Nate kneed him in the back, almost knocking him over.

'Why the hell didn't you ask him?'

The possemen were watching silently now, leery of the sheriff, reading his mood correctly: there was no nonsense about Nate Kendrick this night.

Despite the painful blow, Renny seemed to be the only one who didn't realize his father was on the verge of violent rage.

'You ever tried askin' Frenchy his business, Pa? 'Specially if he don't want to tell you – and that's all the blame time. What's the worry? He'll poke around on his lonesome like he does and I'll bet he'll be right here, holdin' the first cup of java of the day when we wake up.'

Nate cuffed Renny, knocking his hat from his head, and the younger Kendrick stood, angry, but wary, feeling to find out if his hair was ruffled, humiliated. 'The hell's wrong now?'

'Goddamnit, I've been arguin' half the day with that techy old army scout! Reckons someone was ridin' that chestnut we found at Lazy F, says the tracks were too deep for it to have been riderless.'

'Well – maybe it belonged to one of the outlaws we wounded above the pass and he fell off later. Then the damn hoss wandered on down to Lazy F.'

Nate blinked, surprised and impressed by his son's theory. 'Ye-ah. It could've been that way, all right.'

It was Renny's turn to be surprised at his father's reply. Growing more confident, he said, 'What the hell's it matter, anyway? Tess Fowler wouldn't hide no owlhoot. If there'd been a rider, she'd've told us.'

Some of the men murmured agreement, watching Nate. The sheriff still didn't look pleased. He squatted, picked up Renny's mug of coffe and drank from it.

'Cranky old son of a bitch wanted me to leave someone to watch Lazy F. Hell, with the two men we had killed by the outlaws, and the three wounded who just had to go back to town' – Nate said this last through gritted teeth – 'we don't have the men to be scatterin' 'em around now. We can spread out, but always close enough to stay in touch. Leave a man at Lazy F! Judas, he'd be bored stiff or go on down there first time he smelled their grub cookin'.'

'Not Frenchy. He'd stay hid in the middle of a stampede if it was what he wanted to do.'

Nate glared at his son. 'Don't get smart-mouth with me! I'll bet he's gone to watch the damn ranch himself and now we're left without a tracker!'

Renny scratched his chin. 'I can track pretty good, Pa. You told me yourself when we was huntin' deer.'

'Christ, boy, that was years ago! I was just tryin' to make you feel good.' He stood again abruptly, ignoring Renny's slowly protruding lower lip as the hurt sank in in front of the others. 'But we ain't givin' up! Taylor's bunch've gone into a part of the Saddlebacks I know pretty well now. We'll find 'em! And when we do, Cole Adams'll be with 'em! And I want the son of a bitch *alive*! I don't care if he's wounded, long as he's livin'. Our town's gonna have the biggest trial and hangin' ever to hit this neck of the woods. It'll bring in newspapermen from all over the country and that means plenty of rubbernecks'll follow to be there to see Adams swing. We'll put our town on the map!'

'Judas! We'll all be famous!' said someone beyond the glow of the fire, with more than a hint of sarcasm.

Nate Kendrick smiled as they started talking animatedly.

Famous? You bet your britches – and especially me, the lawman who brung Killer Cole Adams to justice!

The recoil from the Frontier Colt kicked Adams's hand up and back, pain searing through his wrist joint. It had suffered some superficial damage when he had been roped to the yoke between the rocks at Taylor's camp. He felt it was much weaker than it had been and he changed the gun over to his other hand.

It too felt the weight dragging at it, but he didn't fire the Colt – he had no intention of trying to shoot left handed: couldn't hit a house from the front porch.

Jimmy Crow had prepared him for this eventuality by cutting two pieces of leather from an old cinch strap, softening them with neatsfoot oil and fitting brass D-rings and straps. The size could easily be adjusted by tightening or loosening the strap passing through the two overlapping D-rings, giving as much or as little support to the wrist as desired.

Cole was high above the ranch here, in the foothills and in a small canyon with a stream. It was far enough away from Lazy F headquarters so that if by some chance the law discovered him, Tess could claim she knew nothing about his presence. Because it had water, he could camp out, stay clear of the ranch for a day or two.

His battered body was healing, but slowly. He was a tough man to attempt the things he was doing but he really did want to get away from Lazy F so that Tess would not be in trouble. He threaded the narrow strap through the rings on the right hand cuff – they were interchangable anyway – and tried several different pressures. The leather firmed against his wrist and was soft enough to follow the contours of the wrist bone and the heel of his hand. He flexed his fingers and it felt good, giving his wrist support. He picked up the heavy Colt and this time had no trouble cocking the hammer with his thumb. Earlier, when he had tried, the gun had fallen from his grip.

He worked at it for several minutes, then stood up, lifted the gun, holding his arm straight out from his shoulder, sighted down the blued steel of the barrel and squeezed the trigger. The gun roared and almost jumped from his hand but he managed to catch it in time. There was pain in the knuckle of his trigger finger but a brief, intense massage got rid of it – something clicked in his knuckle joint so maybe it was only a piece of cartilage that had been squeezed out of position when they had tied him to the sapling.

He would remember every single one of these pains when he caught up with Leith Taylor.

That was what all this was about. Not so much for protecting himself, but working at using his rifle and Colt again in a competent manner for his confrontation with Taylor.

It had to happen.

He should have killed the outlaw years ago. That had been his first mistake; the next was believing that Taylor had been knifed to death in prison. Leith had much too strong a streak of self-preservation to allow that to happen.

When – not if – they met again, he would put things right . . .

By noon he was near exhaustion and made himself rest in the shade, eating some of the cold meat that Tess had packed for him. He was too tired even to brew coffee but he washed the food down with water. He remembered rolling a cigarette but fell asleep before he could light it.

It was late afternoon when he awoke and he was lucky he had been in the shade of a tree and a high boulder, for the sun was still hot and bright.

He felt better for the rest and reloaded the Colt and the rifle as well. Maybe he was getting a mite too ambitious, but he figured that while he felt reasonably fit he might as well use up what energy he had.

By sundown he was shooting the Colt well. The leather wrist cuff was a blessing, though his wrist was beginning to swell some. He eased the cuff and then tried the rifle, folding a couple of large neckerchiefs and pushing them under his shirt at his right shoulder. It was stiff more than sore and he figured it was just muscle strain from having had his arms stretched in the same position for so long when roped to that sapling.

But that first recoil from the rifle had him gasping and swearing. He dropped the Winchester and

121

grabbed at his shoulder, fingers probing and pressing, trying to ease the pain.

It was just beginning to go away when he went very still. *He had heard something!*

He tried to drag his Colt from the holster Jimmy Cross had found for him but fumbled it, just as he heard a rifle lever clash and a harsh voice say,

'You're way too slow, feller. I could beat you with my gun glued in the holster and still have time to roll and light a cigarette. You are *pathetic.* Now you lift them hands high as they'll go or you'll need more'n leather cuffs to make 'em work for you.'

Adams raised his arms slowly, turning his head as he heard the intruder walking across the gravel behind him.

'Well – Chief Scout Lu-cah! It's been a long time since I had you on my trail, Frenchy.'

The old scout frowned, as if trying to remember, but said, 'If I was you, from where you're sittin', I'd be thinkin' it ain't been long enough.'

The rifle barrel swung around and pointed squarely at his chest as Frenchy lifted the weapon to his shoulder and squinted down the barrel.

Then the Winchester sagged a few inches and Frenchy's heavy grey eyebrows arched up towards his hatbrim.

'Wait a minute! What the hell're *you* doin' here? You ain't Cole Adams!'

CHAPTER 12

OLD SCORES

When the trooper finally scaled the cliff and slashed the throat of the Indian on guard, but dozing, at the top, the others were in the process of scalping the scout – alive.

He was doing his best not to scream, but suddenly his mouth opened and out came a terrible blast of agony: with the black hole of the wide-open mouth amongst the rivers of blood running down the weathered old face. It was a horrifying sight – especially with all the slashes and burns on the naked torso and belly.

For a moment, the trooper wasn't sure the scout even still had his symbol of manhood. But then he lifted his Winchester and began picking off the red devils. Sweat streamed from their bodies, naked except for buckskin breech-clouts, and suddenly it was streaked with red. They were deadly shots, spaced, yet swift, and each found its target. No non-fatal wounds, each man fell dead on the spot.

The magazine was empty and there were still two of the savages left, crouching, bloody hatchets ready as their glit-

tering eyes searched for him. He stood up and the Cavalry-issue Remington .44 pistol, with its brass frame gleaming, spat fire and smoke.

The Indians fell writhing on top of the bodies of their companions.

The trooper ran in, pistol back in the button-down holster, clasp knife with blade open, slashing the rawhide bonds that held the scout, sagging and bloody, to the torture post. His half-removed scalp flapped and squished as the trooper swung him over his shoulder and looked for the steep path down that now would be safe to use with all the Indian war-party dead.

'That was a night I'll never forget,' Frenchy Lucas said. He was sipping coffee from a battered tin mug and looking across the coals of the pit camp-fire, which was hidden from prying eyes by rocks that Adams had piled around the hole.

He removed his hat and Adams saw the puckered, scarred skin that covered the first six inches of his head. It was hairless. But other grey-streaked strands, long and untidy, grew around the fringe almost to his shoulders. With his hat on he seemed to have a full head of hair. 'That sawbones you took me to did a good job of sewin' the scalp back into place, but the hair fell out and never grew again on the part of my scalp the varmints lifted.'

'Looks beautiful, Frenchy.'

'Don't care how it looks. I've still got a whole scalp, thanks to you – Trooper Brad Johnson.'

The old eyes studied Cole's still-bruised face.

'That's the name I always associate with that night

them Apaches decided to have some fun with me.'

'Well. You'd promised to get me a bottle of red-eye from the sutler's store at the fort where my credit had run out, and when you never reported in from your scout, I told the captain I'd volunteer to go look for you.'

'Bet he din' argue neither. Not one of the rest of that troop would want to go lookin' for renegade Apaches at night in Injun country – and that includes the captain.'

Adams grinned. 'I really needed that booze, Frenchy.'

'Yeah – well, sorry about that. Injuns drunk your red-eye. Mebbe that's what made 'em act so mean with me.'

'Long time back, Frenchy.' Adams swirled the remains of his coffee around, looking down into the mug. 'Now I can take it or leave it – back then I was ashamed but couldn't help myself.'

'So you used another name.'

'Johnson. Commonest name in the whole U-nited States. I read that in a *Harper's Weekly*.'

'Now you're this Cole Adams, wanted bank robber and killer.' There was a flatness of disapproval in the old tracker's voice, and a query at the same time.

'I'm Cole Adams. I been set up for the other stuff.' He went on to tell his story about Leith Taylor and Frenchy listened in silence, wrenching a hefty chew of tobacco from a grit-sprinkled, sticky hunk. Cole shook his head when Frenchy offered it to him.

'I don't have to tell you you're in real trouble boy.'

'I kinda got that idea.'

'Taylor's a mean son of a bitch. Haven't had much to do with him, 'cept I ran him down for a father whose daughter Taylor raped. He wanted to have the pleasure of turnin' Leith into a eunich – but was the father we found hangin' from a cottonwood – and if he'd been alive he'd've been screamin' in a real high-pitched voice.'

'I need to get him, Frenchy.' Adams hurled the coffee dregs into the coals, which spat and sizzled briefly. 'That damn sheriff's gonna keep me from squaring away my score with Taylor. This is my only chance. I'll never get another. Taylor or Nate Kendrick'll see to that.'

'Nate's got the scent of blood in his nostrils right now,' the tracker admitted. 'Your blood. He can be ornery, old Nate, specially with that boy of his, Renny. There's gonna be one helluva blow-up between 'em one day. I'd like to see it – but preferably through field glasses. Stand too close when it happens and . . .' He shrugged expressively.

Adams rolled a thin cigarette and lit up, flicking his gaze to Lucas's old-leather features. 'As I recall, you made a point of never reporting back to the officers, unless you'd tracked down the quarry.'

Frenchy merely looked at him, spat a stream of tobacco juice to his left. 'Ain't changed. Still got my reputation to keep up.'

'Where does it leave me?'

'Where d'you want it to leave you?'

Cole frowned, not expecting that answer. 'Well – just a bit beyond where I am now – but shooting straight and no trouble handling my guns.'

'Make you up some stuff to smear on them sore spots, includin' your wrists – bar grease with potash an' herbs.'

'No bears around here, Mon-soor Lu-cah.'

The scout grinned, showing a couple of worn yellow stumps. 'Don't have to be – been carryin' a ball of grease wrapped in buckskin for a couple years now.'

'By hell! It must stink!'

Frenchy cackled. 'That's why I never have my saddlebags robbed – one whiff an' anyone with that idea is off like a brush turkey hearin' a hound's howl.'

'Well . . . guess I'm game to try it.' He smoked a little, then said tentatively, 'Whether it works or not, Frenchy, I still need to know where I stand with you.'

'You don't stand nowhere with me.' The grin widened as he saw the puzzlement on Adams's face. Frenchy straightened a gnarled finger and pointed above his head. 'You're up there, somewhere – you have to be, trackin' me through Injun country at night an' tacklin' them Apaches.' He touched his head. 'Wouldn't be here now if you hadn't.'

'I sure needed a drink of whiskey bad that night,' Cole said with a sly grin, and the scout laughed.

'Knew there was some reason you come to save me – thought it musta been my good looks.' The weathered old face straightened and those eyes that had seen a thousand horizons locked with Adams's. 'I'll help you find Taylor. Know the country where we last saw his tracks. Means we'll be lookin' in the same area as Nate's posse, though.'

'Long as we get there first.' Cole Adams held out his right hand. Frenchy took it in his gnarled fist and they shook firmly.

Because of residual pains from his beating, Adams didn't sleep very deeply. He awoke to a very slight sound, much like a moccasined foot being lowered on a dead leaf. He lay still in his bedroll, right hand smeared with Frenchy's vile-smelling unguent, bandaged to help it concentrate its aromatics. Now he closed it around the butt of the Colt he had been holding loosely. His eyes were still closed but he opened them slowly, allowing his sight to accustom itself to what light there was. It was sometime before daylight, he reckoned – or sensed from long years of living outdoors: the camp in the high canyon was grey and blurred.

So was the figure crouching by Frenchy's bedroll, which was closest to the brushline. Cole saw the faint gleam of a rifle barrel, tensed and, hoping the blankets would deaden the sound, slowly cocked the gun hammer.

He was immediately uneasy: a cocked pistol in a bedroll was fraught with danger. Getting it out cleanly was no easy job, and if the hammer spur caught on a tautly drawn blanket, it could easily fire the weapon – against the body of whoever was occupying the bedroll.

But he had to move, and fast. Although it hurt and brought an involuntary grunt from him, he rolled out over the loose side of the blanket, away from the rest of the bed, flopping on his belly. Elbows dug in, he grasped the Colt with both hands and called: 'Hold it right there!'

The man bending over Frenchy rounded as fast as a striking snake, the rifle coming with him, ready to shoot one-handed. Then Frenchy came up out of his roll and crashed a knotted fist under the jaw of the intruder. The man went over backwards and the rifle fired, angled slightly upwards, but sending the bullet close enough to Adams for him to hear the air-whip as it passed.

By the time he had pushed to his feet, Colt still cocked, Frenchy had wrenched the rifle from the other man and now stood over him. He levered in a fresh shell and poked the man with the rifle muzzle.

'Just lie where you are and mebbe you'll live.'

Cole walked across, seeing better now as light grew in the sky, pale pink darkening to crimson in a few minutes, peach-tipped clouds looking as if they were suddenly edged with gold. Despite the scout's warning, the intruder was struggling to prop himself up on his elbows. He gently worked his jaw with one hand.

'By hell, you can punch for an old man!'

Adams knew that voice. 'Don't shoot him, Frenchy! He's Jim Cross, Tess Fowler's ramrod.'

Frenchy muttered profanely. 'Hell almighty! Knew I was losin' my hearin' some, but to be caught in my bedroll by a damn Cherokee 'breed! Don't bear thinkin' about.' He turned his head towards Adams. 'And I'd be mighty obliged if you can forget this ever happened, Cole.'

'Easy. But what about him?' He gestured to Cross.

'No need to worry about him. Part-Cherokees don't like bein' beat by a Blackfoot, neither.'

Cross got slowly and warily to his feet, keeping his hands well away from his gun belt.

'You never "beat" me! Just caught me off-guard. Anyway, thought you was French.'

'Am – kinda. But one of the lady-folk among my ancestors took a shine to a Blackfoot chief who abducted her for a spell.'

'I've heard they do that – use the white women till they get tired of 'em and just leave 'em in the wilds to find their own way out. Or die.'

'Well, they do, most times, but this chief he liked my kinswoman and—'

'When you two are finished discussing your primitive beginnings . . .' Cole said sharply and they looked at him, the scout still covering Cross with the rifle.

'Yeah. What the hell you think you were doin', bendin' over me that way? Gonna slit my throat?'

'Wanted to see who the hell you were. Knew Cole, but when I seen you I remembered you was with Kendrick's posse that come to the Lazy F. Thought you must've captured him.' He broke off to tell Adams: 'Tess was worried about you stayin' out here alone and sent me up to check on you. What's the deal?' He jerked his head towards the old scout. 'Mebbe we can talk better over some hot coffee, eh?'

Jimmy Cross had some sowbelly and beans with him and they cooked it up in his skillet, sat eating it with stale biscuits fried in the grease and sipping coffee. Cole explained briefly how he had known

130

Frenchy in the cavalry some years earlier. The scout lifted his hat and Cross sucked down a sharp breath when he saw the disfigured skin.

'Then you're beholden to Cole.'

'I sure as hell am.'

Cross flicked his gaze from one to the other. 'I guess you got some kind of deal goin'.'

Frenchy told the ramrod to mind his own business but Cole saw no harm in admitting that the scout was going to help him track Leith Taylor.

Cross whistled briefly between his teeth. 'By hell, old Nate won't care for that!'

'What he cares about don't matter a piece of flea-dung to me!'

'It oughta, Frenchy. You gotta live in this county and Nate's mighty touchy – with a long memory.'

Frenchy's reply was to spurt a long stream of tobacco juice over his left arm.

'Jim's right, Frenchy. Might be best if you just point me in the right direction, then go back to the posse.'

Frenchy digested this soberly. 'I know what you done while in the cavalry – but I ain't sure you could tackle Taylor and his three men alone. But if I was to help . . .'

'You want to help me some more?' Adams asked. 'You can, Frenchy: go find Nate – and lead him in the opposite direction!'

'Risky!' said Jimmy Cross. 'But a good idea.'

'Nate won't argue – if you kind of hint it'll save a day he'll have to pay you.'

'One against four ain't the best odds!' protested Cross.

The scout grinned crookedly at Adams before telling the ramrod, 'He climbed a cliff in pitch-dark, killed ten Injuns and brought me back down through Apache country. I like the idea of sashayin' old Nate all over the mountains: it'll give you a better chance at Taylor. You've tangled with him before, so know what to expect. Mebbe it was the need for booze that drove you in those cavalry days, but you got a much stronger motive now to find Taylor and kill him. I'll keep the posse away so you can concentrate on nailin' the bastard.'

But first, Adams had to make sure he could use his guns properly again.

Jimmy Cross left to report to Tess Fowler. With the old scout helping, even massaging his strained shoulder with the stinking bear-grease, by the end of the day Cole was shooting pretty good. He wanted to continue, for there were still a couple of hours of good light left, but Frenchy talked some sense into him and at last he agreed that, OK, he would rest his wrists and shoulder.

The scout carried an old prospector's panning-dish amongst his gear stuffed into extra large canvas saddle-bags. He boiled two coffee pots of water, crushed some rocksalt from his food bag and tipped it into the steaming water, then filled the shallow dish.

'Soak your hands and wrists in that. The heat'll give you relief, and then I'll rub in some more bear-grease.'

'I won't get anywhere near Taylor – he'll smell me coming a mile away!'

132

'When you're feelin' better, jump in a crick, scrub the grease outta your pores with sand.' Frenchy shook his head slowly. 'You sure've gone soft since we rode in the cavalry!'

To save any more arguments, Cole agreed to do as Frenchy suggested. Next morning he felt a lot more mobile and loose-limbed, if still smelling like a rabid grizzly.

In the early light he shot small pigeon-egg-sized pebbles to dust with the rifle, then bounced an empty, rusted coffee can all over their corner of the canyon, using his sixgun. He reloaded with steady hands, ignoring the slight stab of pain from his ribs which Frenchy had bound with several coils of plaited grass-rope.

'I reckon you an' me're just about at the partin' of the ways, Cole. Another day, another week won't make you any more ready than you are now.'

'You'll get no argument from me about that.'

'Then let's ride.'

The country Frenchy had led and goaded the posse through for two gruelling days took less than five hours' hard riding to cross this time.

'Nate'll kill you when he realizes how you stretched your time for a few extra bucks!'

Frenchy laughed, shook his head. 'He'll still need me to find his way back. He won't know where the hell he is if I don't guide him. Renny's a better tracker, but Nate won't have it.'

It was some of the wildest landscape Adams had ever seen, huge geological slips of shale and granite,

133

crumbling spires that reminded him of some illustrations he had once seen in a very thick, leather-bound book printed in Germany. He figured the devil had a hold on this land. Heat beat back from the walls rising on all sides. The horses complained, walking on flint, scattered as thickly as rice at a wedding. A few hardy bushes had found sustenance by probing long root tendrils through cracks in the rock. There were few birds, too, and Cole wondered about water in here, asked the old scout.

He figured Frenchy would know where every drop of naturally stored water was and not long after he had a practical demonstration. Men and mounts all slaked their thirsts at a rock-covered well deep beneath an overhanging ledge.

Afterwards, as the scout's jaws worked on another 'chaw of baccy', and Cole smoked a cigarette, Frenchy said, 'See that canyon way over yonder, a kinda purple haze driftin' through it?' Cole had to shade his eyes but nodded. 'Right through there is Leith Taylor's country – an' I mean that in the sense that it is his. No argument. You try to tell him different and you eat lead. It's where he has his main hole-in-the-wall. You'll find it behind a high, flat redstone wall with a clump of bush near the base. Usually got yaller flowers on it. Or, if no flowers, green buds with a red streak.'

'How the hell do you know this?'

'Once rode down a man used to ride with Leith, got scared off by all the killin'. He weren't a bad feller – someone shot him in the back for a few bucks bounty later. But when I caught him he was scared white. We did a deal: I let him go after he told me where Taylor's hangout was.'

'You've been there?'

'Not me. Well, only far as the red wall. You'll have to find the way in.'

Adams smoked his cigarette down and ground it out beneath his boot. 'You're leaving?'

'Yeah. Time I got back to Nate.' He winked, adding, ' 'Course might take a mite longer to bring the posse here than it took you an' me . . .' He paused, watching Cole, and said, 'You want, I'll still side you.'

Cole thought about it and shook his head. 'You've risked enough, Frenchy, and I'm obliged. I'll take it from here. Realize now it's something been stuck in my craw for a long time. Best put an end to it – and it has to be me does it.'

This time they parted without a handshake, the old scout climbing stiffly into his saddle and flicking Adams a brief salute, knocking dust from his hatbrim. Cole lifted a hand, watched him go, disappearing into the afternoon shadows, then he mounted his horse and checked rifle and sixgun before riding slowly down a steep slope towards a gorge that would be the start of his journey to the distant, hazy canyon.

Where old scores would finally be settled.

For keeps.

CHAPTER 13

TRUE COLOURS

That was it, as far as Renny was concerned. His father had humiliated him in front of the posse for the last time.

All he had done was break away from the line of possemen riding a winding trail around a peak. Renny, without asking Nate's permission – he knew that was behind the sheriff's rage – cut away and set his mount up the steep slope, riding slow zigzags, ignoring calls from Nate to come back, except once when he shouted, 'I'll see better from up high, for Chris'sakes!'

What he had to do on top of the peak took a little longer than expected and it was dark when at last he rode back into the posse's camp – head-on into Nate's anger.

Renny had to stand there and listen to some of the worst epithets he had ever heard his father use. Frustrated with lack of success finding Adams or

Taylor, running up expenses, being harried by the townsmen he had deputized and who now wanted to return to their families, big bounty to share-in notwithstanding, Nate laid into his son relentlessly. Renny made a fine target for Nate but his big mistake was ending the bitter tirade by slapping his son a hard blow across the face.

Every man there sucked down a deep breath – and held it, waiting for the big explosive showdown between father and son they had all – except Nate himself – seen a-brewing for days. They expected Renny – a man not noted for his calmness in the face of insult – even to go for his gun. And, in fact, Renny did instinctively drop his right hand to his Colt, but reason broke through his rage so that he slowly released his hold. He saw the sudden relief on his father's startled face, wanted so badly to punch the ill-tempered sheriff.

Instead, he reached up to his shirt pocket, unpinned his deputy badge and flung it at his father, striking Nate in the chest. The sheriff blinked and stepped back quickly as the badge fell to the ground. 'Wha. . . ? Just what the hell is this? We gonna have a tantrum?' Nate looked around at the silent, sober men. 'Six foot four an' close to two hundred pounds, and he throws a tantrum like a spoiled brat!'

Renny told him in a deceptively calm voice, 'That's my Declaration of Independence, Pa, I'm through with you. No more law work. No more bein' cusssed out by you every time you get a bellyache and I happen to be handy.'

'You watch your mouth, boy!'

137

'Guess I'll have to – 'cause you won't be around to do it.' He nodded to the possemen who looked almost as stunned as Nate and turned to his horse, swinging easily up into the saddle. '*Adios*, all.'

Nate still stood there, jaw dropped a little, eyes pinched, deep creases across his forehead. He watched his son ride away into the darkness and just before Renny disappeared, called,

'When you get lost, fire three shots, break, then fire one more.' With a twisted mouth that lent a sardonic tone to his next words, as if talking to a naughty child, Nate added, 'Don't you worry none, we'll come a'runnin', find you and lead you out by the hand!'

It unsettled him to hear Renny's laughter drift in out of the darkness beyond the glow of the camp-fire.

'Mebbe you'll be the one to get lost, Pa. I'm damn sure I won't!'

Nate Kendrick glanced around at the others, truly puzzled.

'Now what the hell did he mean by that? He don't know this country any better'n the rest of us.'

But some of the smarter ones in the posse figured that Nate was forgetting Renny knew enough to ride up that peak so as to get an overview of what lay ahead.

But, of course, the sheriff had never even asked about what Renny saw – he was too set on taking out his foul mood on his son.

An hour later, when the posse was turning in for the night, Frenchy Lucas rode into the camp.

Nate had been very quiet and surly since Renny's departure and he started up again by berating the scout. 'You took your blamed time! Wanderin' all over the country instead of reportin' back in, pronto! Hell, you knew the posse was desperate for a sure lead . . .'

'That I can't give you, Nate,' Frenchy replied evenly enough, standing by his weary horse. 'But I reckon I might have a general direction – seen some camp-fire smoke. Could've been Adams, or maybe Taylor's outfit. Mebbe they've joined up again by now.'

Nate stared, slowly forcing himself to speak civilly. 'Well – I guess it's a start. More than we had to go on. Might be some coffee still warm.'

Frenchy shook his head, pulled out his chewing-tobacco and bit into what was left of it. The posse didn't show a lot of interest because they knew now that the sheriff would have them on the trail early, following the old tracker to where he had seen the camp-fire smoke.

Nate sat on a log just out of the firelight, watching Frenchy lay out his old mangy-looking bearskin bedroll, getting ready to turn in. Quietly, Kendrick called to him, 'You notice Renny ain't here?'

'I noticed.'

'Dunno what the hell's wrong with him but he tossed in his badge earlier, quit the posse.'

Frenchy pursed his lips thoughtfully, but made no comment.

Nate sighed. 'I know you been leadin' us all over the place, holdin' things up so's I'll have to pay you

139

more.' He paused, expecting the scout to deny it but Frenchy said nothing, his expression unchanged. 'OK. Forget that. I . . . I want you to draw me a rough map of where you spotted that smoke.'

'It'll be rough all right if I draw it.'

The sheriff held up a hand. 'Anything'll do, long as it points us in the general direction.'

'Don't need a map. I'll take you there.'

'No. Want you to do somethin' else for me.' He fidgeted, obviously uncomfortable about what he was going to say. 'I'll lift your daily pay by . . . half, fifty per cent raise . . . if you'll find Renny and bring him back.'

He was breathing hard and Frenchy stayed silent for a long, drawn-out minute. 'So's you can cuss him out again?'

'No, goddammit!' Nate gritted, trying to keep his voice low. 'I – I've had a dirty liver or somethin' with Renny lately. Said some things earlier I shouldn't ought've.'

'And held him on too tight a rein for too damn long. He was bound to kick over the traces sooner or later.'

'I din' ask your opinion! You want the extra pay or not?'

'Sure I do. Whether I bring Renny back or don't?'

'Judas, you drive a hard bargain! No, *no*, damned if I'll be blackmailed. Two days. That's how long you got to find him and bring him in. Otherwise, you just come back.'

'If I feel so inclined.'

The sheriff frowned. 'You better! Or you don't get paid at all.'

Frenchy spat a stream. 'Always a pleasure doin' business with you, Nate.'

Mid-morning, Frenchy Lucas squatted, studying the ground amongst some sparse timber, lifted his hatbrim and scratched at his scarred scalp.

'Well, I'll be! He's tryin' to cover his tracks!'

The old scout had suspected it a little way back along the winding trail that Renny had left. There was sign that made him think the deputy – ex-deputy now – was trying to hide his tracks – and here he was, staring at ground that showed no tracks at all. Suddenly. As if the man's horse had started to fly.

All sorts of theories began to form in Lucas's head as he straightened, kink by kink, easing rheumaticky joints.

'Looks like he means it this time – not comin' back to Poppa no matter what. But where the hell is he goin'?'

Frenchy moved out to the edge of the timber and scanned the country within his arc of vision. He stiffened slightly when he saw the hint of that purple haze that always seemed to hang over Leith Taylor's hidden canyon.

'By Godfrey! I wonder! Somebody had to tell Taylor the best time to hit the stages or banks! Nate won't let . . .'

Something smashed into his back, high between the shoulder blades, slamming him against his horse which shied away. The oldster sprawled on the ground, his face pushed into the earth, screwed up in pain. He heard the dying echoes of a gunshot and

141

thought, as a gout of blood leapt from his mouth, that it was likely from the gun that had shot him.

As his vision blurred, he watched a man step out from behind a tree, smoking rifle in his hands. The Winchester lifted to the man's shoulder and just as the dying scout recognized him, it fired.

This time Frenchy Lucas never heard the sound of the shot that killed him.

Tess Fowler reined down her buckskin mount and looked sharply at Jimmy Cross as he pulled up alongside her.

'Are we lost, Jimmy?' She looked and sounded annoyed.

'I – no, we're not lost, Tess, but I warned you when you insisted on ridin' out here, that I might not be able to find their tracks.'

'You found their camp. They would have pushed on at sun-up, so they should've left tracks!'

'That Frenchy – claims he's part Blackfoot and I believe it. I ain't boastin' but I'm pretty good at trackin' an' hidin' my sign, but that damn old scout – he leaves me for dead.'

Tess' angry face didn't soften. 'We're wasting time!'

'I told you, Cole's OK – looks a lot fitter than when he left Lazy F. And that's Frenchy's doin', too. He's safe as he'll ever be, long as he has that old scout for a sidekick.'

She compressed her lips and her shoulders sagged out of the stiff angry line they had been holding. 'I knew this would happen. I should never have agreed for him to camp out while he supposedly practised with his guns.'

'Aw, he'd been doin' that. Was the gunfire that led me to 'em as much as anythin' else.'

She continued as if he hadn't spoken: 'I knew as soon as he felt he could pull the trigger and hit what he was aiming at that he would go after Leith Taylor! I knew it and yet I – I was stupid enough to give in to his badgering.'

Jimmy smiled faintly. 'Met your match at last for stubbornness, eh, Tess?'

Her eyes flared angrily but she choked down the outburst that sprang to her lips. She even smiled a little, shook a finger at the amused Cross.

'Now only you could get away with talking to me like that, Jimmy Cross! You're taking advantage of your position.'

'Nope. Just defendin' myself. 'Cause whatever you think, better men than me've tried to track Frenchy Lucas when he didn't want 'em to and had no more success than me.'

'Oh, all right! We've been riding too long. I feel gritty and sweaty and I'm hungry and badly want a decent cup of coffee.'

He started to dismount. 'Well, that last part's easy. All we gotta do is build a fire.'

She was going to protest but reason made her swallow her impatience and she began to feel a mite embarrassed at showing so plainly her concern for the welfare and safety of Cole Adams. After all, while she believed him innocent of the crimes he was being blamed for, he was still only a drifter – wasn't he?

And what difference does that make? she asked herself.

She must have spoken aloud for Cross, lighting tinder for the fire, glanced up and asked, 'You say somethin'?'

'No – I was – just telling my horse to settle down – I'll grind some coffee beans.'

'*Bueno*! A cup of java made with fresh-ground beans is just what I need!'

Both Tess and Jimmy Cross snapped their heads up at the sound of the voice. The ramrod saw Renny Kendrick grin coldly as he levered a shell into his rifle.

'Tess! *Run*!' Cross yelled, leaping up and kicking the burning tinder in Renny's direction.

Kendrick jumped away instinctively and the rifle exploded, the bullet burning across the rump of Tess's buckskin. It reared and whinnied, pawing the air, laid back its ears and ran for the trees.

Jimmy Cross dived for the ground, dragging his sixgun free. He hit hard on his chest, yelling again to the frozen girl: '*Run like hell!*'

Rolling over and over he began firing at Renny who dodged behind a tree. Tess turned to run and fell over the saddlebag she had off-loaded so as to get the coffee beans and hand grinder. Renny's rifle cracked and dirt kicked into Cross' eyes. He yelled in pain, clawed at his face, writhing.

Renny fired two shots into him and the ramrod jerked, then lay still, blood on his shirt front. Tess was up and starting to run and Renny laughed briefly as he put a bullet into the ground between her pounding half-boots. She gave a small cry, stumbled, and tried to regain her balance.

But he leapt towards her and she felt the iron grip of his fingers digging into her arm. He shook her roughly, her hat falling off, hair flying wild.

'Now you just stay put, ma'am. I still want that cup of java!'

He flung Tess roughly and she sprawled on the ground, close to Cross who lay, unmoving, his blood soaking into the dry earth.

Renny pulled a dirty-looking plug of chewing-tobacco from his pocket, bit off a chew, then spat it out, tossing the rest away. 'Stinks as bad as that old scout himself!'

CHAPTER 14

RED RECKONING

Cole Adams rode warily out of the canyon country he had been reconnoitring when he heard the echoes of distant gunfire for the second time.

The first, long before these new sounds, had been only a single shot. It might have been a hunter, or even a posseman, killing something for the pot, and he pushed it to the back of his mind. It had been a long way off.

He was impatient to find his way to Taylor's camp – it was much harder than he had thought – and he had been well within sight of the red wall Frenchy had told him about when the second blast of gunshots reached him. The single shot he could dismiss, but this was a crackle of several, irregular shots. *A gunfight? Brief, but how many bullets did it take to kill a man. . . ?*

In this country, riding into hell knew what kind of danger, he knew what lay behind him was as important as what lay ahead, in case he ended up sand-wiched between two enemies.

Reluctantly, he started back the way he had come.

His horse sensed the presence of the second animal before he heard its low whinny. He tightened his grip on the rifle, cocked and ready to fire. Then he saw the pale flash of colour through the brush and let his mount walk in towards it.

Something cold gripped his belly as he recognized Tess's buckskin – and the bleeding gash across its rump. The animal was approachable enough, no doubt relieved to find some friendly creatures, and, close up, he saw that the wound was from a bullet. Not serious, but enough to send the horse running in panic.

He dismounted, calmed the buckskin, then checked the one remaining saddle-bag. His worst fears were confirmed: he recognized some of the contents as belonging to Tess Fowler.

He ground-hitched both horses, walked down to where the buckskin had first appeared, and began searching for tracks.

Jimmy Cross still had a spark of life left in him; he groaned as the kneeling Adams tilted his canteen against the blood-flecked lips. His eyelids seemed too heavy to raise, but his glazing eyes showed a little recognition.

'What the hell happened, Jim? Is Tess all right. . . ?' It took some time for Cross to work up the strength to make any kind of a reply. Most of it was garbled and grunted, interspersed with heavy,

147

laboured breathing but eventually Cole managed to understand.

'Renny – shot me – took Tess – Gone loco . . .'

'Renny? No sign of the rest of the posse?'

Cross rolled his head painfully from side to side, worked one hand along the ground, curling it into a half-fist and pointed with a shaky forefinger.

As Jimmy's eyes closed for the last time, Cole saw what he was trying to draw his attention to.

A sticky plug of chewing tobacco that he recognized instantly. A cold shiver streaked down his spine and in his mind he heard again that distant, single rifle shot.

But Renny Kendrick running wild? He had a mean streak but to Adams he had seemed well and truly under Nate's thumb. He couldn't picture him as a loner on the prod.

But he was more than that right now! He had Tess.

The ramrod's horse was missing and Cole figured Tess would be riding it since her own had run off. So, he wrapped Jimmy Cross's body in the ramrod's blanket, draped it across the packhorse, roping it in place. He unhitched the nervy animal and slapped it across the rump with his hat.

It would find its way back to Lazy F.

He scouted around, found where Renny had watched Tess and Cross from behind a tree. If he was right in his suspicions that Renny had already killed old Frenchy there was no profit to anyone in back-tracking.

So he spent time that made his stomach knot with barely controlled impatience searching for tracks he could follow. He studied the hoofmarks of Renny's mount where it had been tied to a tree, also the sign left by Jimmy Cross's claybank, small imperfections that individualized each track.

A spreading, circular search eventually led him in the direction Renny had taken with Tess. He had hurriedly tried to wipe out the sign but the cavalry trained its men well and Adams had never forgotten the lessons in tracking. Also Frenchy had passed on some of his vast knowledge of the art.

It took him a little time to figure out Renny's method of covering his tracks and then he looked for sign indicating this and travelled the faster.

The only surprise was that it was leading him back into the wild canyon country where Frenchy claimed Leith Taylor's outfit hung out.

The outlaw boss stood outside his ramshackle hut, hipshot, thumbs hooked into his slanting gun belt, right hand gloved as usual.

Crewe was standing a little off to the left, a rifle in hand, watching Renny Kendrick ride across the meadow with Tess Fowler tied to Jimmy Cross's claybank. A third outlaw, Linus Taft, sat nearby on a log, his sixgun in his hand.

No one spoke until Renny rode up and stopped a few yards away.

'Lando let you pass?' asked Taft.

'Wouldn't've got this far if he hadn't,' Taylor said sharply, his eyes on the girl, already undressing her in his mind. 'You brung me a present, Renny?'

Renny, more nervous than he'd figured he would

be, nodded eagerly. 'Figured you might like to have some fun – while you're waitin' for Adams to show.'

All three outlaws stiffened. Crewe stepped forward, a threat in his manner and voice. 'You told him how to get here?'

Renny was already shaking his head before Crewe had finished the question. 'That old scout was leadin' him in – pointed him in the right direction and was on his way back to rejoin the posse, I reckon, when I – met him.' They waited and he licked his lips, nodding emphatically. 'He's dead now.'

Tess's lips compressed and she kicked her heels into the claybank's flanks, making it jump into Renny's sorrel. He almost fell from the saddle and rounded on her angrily, but stopped the blow he was intending to deliver, when Taylor laughed.

'Love a gal with spirit! OK, Crewe picked up your mirror flash from Tonto Peak. We been waitin' for you.'

'Had to cover my tracks.' Renny looked sly, adding, 'Just left enough for Adams to find, make sure he don't lose his way.'

Taft frowned and looked at Crewe who shrugged but Taylor, slightly surprised, nodded approval. 'You did good, Renny. Only thing is, now you've quit we won't have no one to tell us when there's an express box on the stage worth stealin' or when a train's carryin' a payroll, or a bank's safe is loaded. Feedin' us that info made us a lotta money.'

Renny's chest swelled a little. 'Well, I was in a good position to know. They were always askin' us to make sure the route would be safe and so on; had to give

150

us the timetables, too.' He touched his hip pocket on the left-hand side. 'Got a couple here oughta see us through a couple new jobs – while you're waitin' to collect the bounty on Adams.'

'And your old man never suspected?'

'Nah. Too busy lookin' for fault with my general work.' His face straightened and for a moment Tess was surprised to see a flash of puzzled hurt in the big man's eyes. 'Still dunno why he had his knife into me – all my life he hammered me down. I'm twenty-seven, and he treats me like a kid—'

'OK, we don't need your family history,' Taylor growled, stepping closer to look up at Tess. He grinned, placed a hand on her thigh where her riding Levis were stretched taut. But only her hands were tied to the saddle horn and she immediately kicked him in the face.

Taylor staggered back, tasting blood, his eyes blazing when he saw the redness on the tips of the fingers he put to his mouth. The others were tensed, expectant. Leith Taylor surprised them all by smiling, teeth smeared with blood. He patted Tess's knee and stepped away hurriedly.

'You'll do me, lady! You got no idea what fun we're gonna have before I'm finished with you!'

She was white now, tried to restrain the trembling she felt trying to take over her body. Taylor scared her! The more she resisted him, the better he seemed to like it . . .

Dabbing at his split lip, Taylor spoke to Taft and Crewe. 'Get her into the hut. Keep her hands tied and rope her to the end of my bunk.' As the outlaws moved to obey, Tess kicking and struggling as best she could, Leith turned to Renny. 'Best step on down. When can we expect Adams?'

'Dunno for sure, but he's no fool, and that old scout taught him plenty. He could be here tonight, but more likely sun-up,' Renny said as he dismounted. He felt more confident and relaxed now that Taylor had approved his move. 'I hope you been keepin' my share of the profits safe.'

Taylor's face was momentarily blank, then he nodded, clapping an arm across Kenny's wide shoulders.

'All safe an' sound, Renny. You're really shakin' old Nate this time, huh?'

'Damn right! Put up with enough and this seemed like a good time. I mean, we can clear out, with Adams dead or alive, to claim the big bounty, and the Old Man can chalk up another unsuccessful posse! Town'll never elect the old bastard again!'

Taylor nodded: Renny was deeply involved in his revenge on his father for all the wrongs – real or fancied, though mostly real – he had endured over the years. That was good: it was an easy subject to use as a diversion when an awkward answer was required for one of Renny's questions.

'We got us some red-eye – real stuff, not moonshine. We can have ourselves a little celebration, mebbe pass the gal around. I don't mind second-hand goods.'

'Suits me – but what about if Adams shows?'

'Lando's on guard. He'll stay there all night. If Adams shows durin' that time he won't know what hit him. But, one thing: I've told the others and now I'm tellin' you: no matter what, *I want Cole Adams alive!* The man who kills him before I've had my fun with him will wish he'd never been born.'

Renny gulped, trying to cover the sound. 'Whatever you say, Leith.'

'Stay with that.'

Renny Kendrick and Taylor had underestimated Cole Adams.

He came within sight of the red wall an hour before sundown, the reflected light like blood at one stage before the angle of the rays changed and it settled to a deep amber.

He had left his horse ground-hitched on the far side of a clump of boulders, the base of which was wreathed with a belt of bushes the mount could browse over to keep it quiet. Once he was certain that Renny was indeed headed for the red canyon, Cole hadn't bothered with the laborious chore of checking for the ex-deputy's sign. He had come straight here by the trails Frenchy had told him about and which he had been following earlier when he had heard the distant gunfire.

Now, afoot, rifle ready in his hands, he crouched at the edge of the thinned-out timber, seeing the stumps now with old axe marks, telling him the outlaws had cleared the trees so as to make the approach difficult for an enemy.

Well, he was an enemy and, now he had figured things out, he lay in a patch of deep shadow, forcing down the urge to run forward and search for the entrance. He was watching for a guard; if Taylor's bunch had taken all this trouble to protect their hideout, there would have to be a guard.

But he was damn hard to see.

Adams calculated about fifteen minutes had passed since his arrival and he had not yet seen any sign of a man on guard. *There had to be one!* It was tempting to take things at face value and step into the open to look for the entrance, but it could also be fatal.

He was about to change position when he saw something up near where the rim curved. At first he thought it was a bird, then, heart hammering, realized that it was part of a man's hat, moving as he changed position. No! It wasn't even that – it was the *shadow* of a man's hat, thrown by the westering sunlight on to the opposite curve of the rim.

Cole shifted his gaze slowly, following the rim inch by inch – and there was the guard. Reclining in an easy position on a short, narrow ledge, likely padded with old blankets. It was a wonder the man hadn't fallen asleep.

Or maybe he had, was just turning over to get his hips in a more comfortable position. It would be a boring chore and if Renny had passed this way earlier the guard would likely have been alert for a while, then bordeom would have crept back and he had dozed.

It was a chance loaded with danger. If he was wrong, was spotted . . .

But he had to get into the hideout before it was dark. He would have no hope of finding the hidden entrance once night fell. Frenchy had said it seemed to him that the red wall was impossible for a man to climb. Looking at the flat rock, crimson again now in the sundown light, Adams had to admit that even a lizard would have trouble going up that way.

Frenchy had never seen any other wall but the red one. Cole figured the wall had to end somewhere, curve down again, or fall into a slope, studded with either bushes or rocks a man could use for a foothold. Or cover.

The shadow where he lay hidden was moving slowly, narrowing into a band that would eventually expose him. So he had to move soon in any case. Right now seemed the best option. Easing back was the only way to go: forward and he would be in that deep amber light, an easy target for the man above.

He couldn't assume the man was asleep, or even dozing. So he snaked his way back on his belly, careful not to snag the rifle. Inch by inch – then six inches at a time – a foot – and, finally, to a tree thick enough to hide him if he stood. Hat now hanging down his back by the leather tie-thong, rifle held vertical, flat against the rough bark of the tree, he searched as far as he could see – and swore when he realized that the first of that mysterious purple haze that covered the red wall for most of the time was thickening with the approaching sundown.

Use it, you fool! It's perfect cover!

And it was. He had to place his feet carefully, avoiding dead leaves and twigs and gravel, but he was able to make his way along to the right where he thought he had seen the suggestion of a shadowy line curving down towards the canyon floor before the mist had blurred things.

He was sweating, although the mist was clammy, the metal of the rifle barrel coated with a kind of dew. Fingertips dragging lightly along the red rock wall, he felt his way through the mist. His throat and nostrils were itching a little and he hoped he wouldn't sneeze or cough.

And suddenly there was no rock at his fingertips. He cautiously felt around but had to lean in that direction before he encountered anything solid. It was dirt! With stumpy grass. A little more exploration and he realized that the rock wall had ended and the broken mountain slope beyond was studded with sparse bush.

Best of all, the ground sloped upwards, rising towards the top of the red wall. A long way up – he couldn't see very far in the mist – but he slipped the rifle through his belt at the back and used both hands and carefully placed boots to make the climb.

He made frequent stops when he fought to get his breathing under control. Rasping breath had given away many a man having to expend a lot of effort to creep up on the enemy. But, despite his moving silently, the guard heard him. Maybe he had come fully awake when the clammy mist had started to settle on him. Whatever the reason, the man suddenly rose up in front of Adams, a bare yard away. The rifle started to come up and Cole grabbed for the breech, locking his hand over the cocked hammer so the gun couldn't fire. The startled guard tugged and fought and Adams kicked him savagely in the shins. The man, Lando, grunted in pain and released the weapon. Cole lowered the hammer even as he brought the brass buttplate up, cracking against Lando's jaw. The man started to collapse and Cole kicked him in the back of the leg. It folded, and with a gargling cry, muffled by the fog, Lando pitched off the high wall.

For a long time later, Cole Adams would awake in the middle of the night, hearing that squishing, bone-snapping sound as the man struck the rocks below. Head first.

He dropped Lando's rifle and took his own from his belt. Now all he had to do was find a way down the *inside* of the red wall and into Taylor's hidden canyon.

There was still enough light to locate the path used by the men coming to stand guard duty at the wall. He saw the crude huts, recognized Jimmy Cross's claybank and Renny Kendricks' mount. He thought he could hear voices, shouting, singing, maybe. And then a man he recognized as Linus Taft from when they had beaten him up, lurched outside and urinated.

He went icy cold. Tess must be inside there. With a bunch of drunken outlaws – Taylor no doubt egging them on to . . . *He didn't want to think beyond that! Surely it wasn't going to happen again! Not twice in one man's life! He couldn't arrive too late this time!*

So, with no time to lose, Cole, crouching, worked around so that the swaying, chuckling Taft had his back to him. Cole knew he had made a little noise but Taft seemed too drunk and too busy to hear it.

157

Then he stopped, turned to look over his shoulder – just in time to catch the butt of Cole's rifle between the eyes.

He dropped like a tree after the final axe blow.

The racket from the hut quietened a little and a slurred voice called, 'Hey, Taft! Don't wash the mountain away!'

Laughter and – he froze, sure his heart had stopped beating – a woman cried out in obvious pain.

'*Tess!*'

The word leapt from his throat as he stepped into the doorway, rifle braced at his hip, working lever and trigger in a blasting volley. Gunsmoke shrouded the moving figures but he had seen that Tess was on the bunk, arms tied over her head.

He directed the gunfire to the left and Crewe, bringing up a sawn-off shotgun, lifted to his toes, his throat shot away in a bloody mess, head hanging by a shred. The shotgun went off, blasting its load of buckshot into the floor, causing Renny Kendrick, who was already wounded, to stagger to one side, bringing up his Colt.

Cole shot him down and then the magazine was empty. He dropped the hot Winchester instantly, palmed up his Colt and saw Taylor bending over Tess, one hand pressed into his side. There was blood on Tess's semi-nude body, too, but Cole didn't know whether it was hers or from Taylor, now holding his pistol to her head. Cole tried not to look at the terror in her eyes as she silently appealed to him.

'Seems almost like this has happened before,

don't it, Adams?' Taylor spoke harshly and there were a few gasps between the words. Cole knew the man's wound was hurting. *Hurting like hell, he hoped.*

'Not this time, Taylor. You were lucky last time. You don't get a second chance.'

'Shoot me and she's dead!'

'I said no second chance!'

The hut's walls seemed to shudder with the blast of the Colt and the bullet hit just where Cole had aimed: high in the left shoulder, about level with the collar bone, wrenching Taylor violently away from the bunk. His gun arm instinctively swung up wildly for balance, driving a bullet into the wall far above Tess.

Taylor sobbed in excruciating pain – the bullet had shattered his collar bone – and he was down on one knee, his face a dreadful sallow grey. He forced the pain down, looking bleakly and contemptuously at Adams, at the same time, trying to bring up his Colt and turn it towards Tess.

Cole's face was cold and expressionless as he shot Taylor twice, once in the groin, once in the side of the head.

He stepped over the twitching body, untied the sobbing girl and dragged a blanket off a bunk so she could cover her nakedness. She clung to him so tightly he had trouble keeping balance. Arms folded about her quivering body, he led her to a chair and sat her in it.

'Sorry you had to see that.'

She rolled her reddened eyes towards him and even half-smiled; it must have hurt her swollen, bruised face.

'I – only wish – I – I'd done it.'

She broke down again and he threw a saddle blanket over the mess that had been Crewe, pulled his chair up beside her and sat with his arm around her, letting her cry it out.

Yet when she paused, looked up with tear-stained face, it was him she was thinking of.

'You – you can never prove you – weren't in all those – robberies and killings – now.'

He smiled thinly. 'I left one alive outside. Linus Taft, I think his name is. He don't have much guts. He'll talk if it'll save his neck being stretched.'

'I hope so. Then what will you do?'

'Go back to prospecting or maybe ranch work.' He held her gaze and he could see her thinking about his words through the pain she must be suffering. He stood suddenly. 'I'll make some coffee and we'll move into one of the other huts.'

She reached for his hand, stopping him as he made to turn towards the stove.

'Lazy F needs an extra hand – or, maybe "needs" isn't quite the right word – wants an extra hand might be better.'

He was briefly silent, then said, deadpan, 'I guess you oughta know – you're the boss.'

Her laughter, brief though it was, was the sweetest sound he'd heard in years.